*He didn't kn____
didn't know ____
he'd never felt so alone in his
life.*

Mark leaned back in his chair, his thoughts
drifting to April. Something about her touched
him. Something about her pierced through the
echo of loneliness in his heart and filled him
with the promise of possibility.

He wanted her. And though he knew little about
her, he wanted her as he hadn't wanted a woman
in a very long time.

But Mark knew he'd be a fool to follow through
on the desire he felt for her. He was playing a
role. He had a killer to catch, a ranch to save,
and that had to take precedence over anything
else in his life.

Most especially what he felt for April.

Dear Reader,

This is officially "Get Caught Reading" month, so why not get caught reading one—or all!—of this month's Intimate Moments books? We've got six you won't be able to resist.

In *Whitelaw's Wedding,* Beverly Barton continues her popular miniseries THE PROTECTORS. Where does the Dundee Security Agency come up with such great guys—and where can I find one in real life? A YEAR OF LOVING DANGEROUSLY is almost over, but not before you read about *Cinderella's Secret Agent,* from Ingrid Weaver. Then come back next month, when Sharon Sala wraps things up in her signature compelling style.

Carla Cassidy offers a *Man on a Mission,* part of THE DELANEY HEIRS, her newest miniseries. Candace Irvin once again demonstrates her deft way with a military romance with *In Close Quarters,* while Claire King returns with a *Renegade with a Badge* who you won't be able to pass up. Finally, join Nina Bruhns for *Warrior's Bride,* a romance with a distinctly Native American feel.

And, of course, come back next month as the excitement continues in Intimate Moments, home of your favorite authors and the best in romantic reading.

Leslie J. Wainger
Executive Senior Editor

Please address questions and book requests to:
Silhouette Reader Service
U.S.: 3010 Walden Ave., P.O. Box 1325, Buffalo, NY 14269
Canadian: P.O. Box 609, Fort Erie, Ont. L2A 5X3

Man on a Mission
CARLA CASSIDY

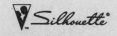

INTIMATE MOMENTS™

Published by Silhouette Books

America's Publisher of Contemporary Romance

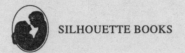 SILHOUETTE BOOKS

ISBN 0-373-27147-6

MAN ON A MISSION

Printed in U.S.A.

Books by Carla Cassidy

Silhouette Intimate Moments

One of the Good Guys #531
Try To Remember #560
Fugitive Father #604
Behind Closed Doors #778
†*Reluctant Wife* #850
†*Reluctant Dad* #856
‡*Her Counterfeit Husband* #885
‡*Code Name: Cowboy* #902
‡*Rodeo Dad* #934
In a Heartbeat #1005
‡*Imminent Danger* #1018
Strangers When We Married #1046
††*Man on a Mission* #1077

Silhouette Desire

A Fleeting Moment #784
Under the Boardwalk #882

Silhouette Shadows

Swamp Secrets #4
Heart of the Beast #11
Silent Screams #25
Mystery Child #61

Silhouette Yours Truly

Pop Goes the Question

Silhouette Books

Shadows 1993
"Devil and the Deep Blue Sea"

Silhouette Romance

Patchwork Family #818
Whatever Alex Wants... #856
Fire and Spice #884
Homespun Hearts #905
Golden Girl #924
Something New #942
Pixie Dust #958
The Littlest Matchmaker #978
The Marriage Scheme #996
Anything for Danny #1048
Deputy Daddy #1141
Mom in the Making #1147
An Impromptu Proposal #1152
Daddy on the Run #1158
Pregnant with His Child... #1259
*Will You Give My Mommy
   a Baby?* #1315
‡*Wife for a Week* #1400
*The Princess's White
   Knight* #1415
Waiting for the Wedding #1426
Just One Kiss #1496
Lost In His Arms #1514

The Loop

Getting it Right: Jessica

*The Baker Brood
†Sisters
‡Mustang, Montana
††The Delaney Heirs

CARLA CASSIDY

has written over thirty-five books for Silhouette. In 1995, she won Best Silhouette Romance, and in 1998, she won a Career Achievement Award for Best Innovative Series, both from *Romantic Times Magazine*.

Carla believes the only thing better than a good book to read is a good story to write. She's looking forward to writing many more and bringing hours of pleasure to readers.

Prologue

"How's he doing?" Johnna Delaney asked, her voice a hushed whisper in the hospital room.

"The doctor says he's going to be all right physically." Matthew Delaney's voice was also low, barely audible.

"And mentally?" Johnna asked.

There was a long pause. "It's too early to tell. He took quite a blow to the head. There's a possibility he might have suffered brain damage."

Their voices drifted away, letting Mark Delaney know they had left his hospital room. He opened his eyes and turned his head toward the brilliant morning sun dancing into the window.

For the first time in the four days since he'd been brought into the hospital with a severe head injury, he felt completely lucid.

And with the lucidness came memories. Marietta

passing him a note in secret. "Meet me at the barn at midnight tonight. It's important."

And he had met her at the barn at midnight. The moon had been full as he'd stood just outside the barn awaiting her approach. He couldn't imagine what the pretty social director on his family ranch wanted to discuss with him. All her dealings were usually with his father, Adam.

He saw her then, hurrying toward him. "Hey, handsome," she said, greeting him in her familiar fashion, but her trademark smile was absent, replaced by a frown of worry.

"Hey, gorgeous," he responded. He and Marietta enjoyed an easy, flirtatious relationship based on the mutual knowledge that there was no real chemistry—other than friendship—between them.

"Thank you for meeting me." She reached a hand out for his, as if she needed the physical contact. Mark realized as he gripped her hand that it wasn't just worry that darkened her eyes, but fear.

"Marietta, what's wrong? What's going on? Why did you want to meet out here in the middle of the night?"

"I don't want anyone to know I've spoken with you."

"Spoken with me about what?"

"Before I say anything, you have to promise me something," she said.

"What?"

"Promise me you won't say anything to anyone. Not your brothers, not your sister...nobody." She squeezed his hand tightly. "I don't know who to trust—and I don't know who you can trust. I'm taking a chance in trusting you, but I have to say something to somebody.''

''I don't understand—''

''Promise me,'' she repeated fervently.

''Okay, I promise. Now, what's going on?''

''Something bad is going on here at the ranch. Something very bad.''

''What do you mean 'bad'?'' Mark pressed. ''If it's something illegal, we'll go to Sheriff Broder.''

''No! I'm not sure that he's not involved,'' she protested. ''I've heard whispers…rumors. What they're doing is wrong…illegal and eventually will destroy us all.'' Her voice rose hysterically with each word.

Mark released her hand and grabbed her by the shoulders. ''Marietta, calm down. Now, tell me who is doing what?''

He saw her eyes widen and fill with sheer terror. Before he realized what caused her fear, he felt a blow to the back of his head—one second of excruciating pain, then complete and total blackness.

Mark now pulled himself up to a sitting position in the hospital bed, rage battling with grief as he thought of the events that had led to his hospitalization and Marietta's death.

Somebody had killed her and tried to kill him. Somebody had sneaked up behind him and silenced Marietta before she could tell him exactly what was going on.

He tossed back the covers and stood, pleased to discover no headache and no unsteadiness as he made his way across the room to the window.

In fact, what he felt more than anything was a relentless energy, a need to get out of this hospital and find out what secret Marietta knew. The secret that had gotten her killed.

"Mark!" He whirled around to see his brother and sister standing in the doorway. "You're up. Thank God." Matthew stalked across the floor and peered at him intently. "How are you feeling? You doing okay? Everyone has been really anxious to talk to you, to find out what happened."

Promise me. Marietta's words spun in Mark's head. *Promise me you won't say anything to anyone. Not your brothers, not your sister…nobody. I don't know who to trust.*

"I'm okay," Mark replied.

"Can you tell us what happened?"

He sensed the intensity in Matthew's voice, and suspicion bloomed. What *was* going on at the ranch? Who was involved? Marietta had said it was bad, illegal. She'd implied he should not trust not only his own family but the sheriff, as well.

"Mark?" Matthew pressed.

Mark raked a hand through his hair, unsure how to reply.

"Stop it, Matthew," Johnna said. "You're obviously upsetting him. We'll have time to talk when he's feeling stronger."

"I feel fine," Mark said, his mind working to assess how best to handle the entire situation. He needed to buy some time, needed to think about what had happened, the things Marietta had implied.

Brain damage. The two words flirted around the edge of his subconscious. Perhaps he could buy himself a little bit of time, pretend his brain wasn't working quite right, until he could figure out exactly what was going on.

Trust nobody. Not his family, not law enforcement. Marietta's words haunted him, and he knew he was on his own to find out what was going on at the ranch and who had killed her and why.

Chapter 1

"There must be some mistake." The tall, dark-haired man looked at April Cartwright as if she were a dead fly that had accidentally fallen on his shirt. "There are no available jobs here."

"But that's impossible," April protested. She cast a quick glance at her car where her eleven-year-old son, Brian, was waiting, then looked back at the man before her. "I finalized the arrangement with Adam Delaney last week. He knew I was arriving today. I'm to be the new social director."

Could he hear her heart pounding? Could he sense her desperation? Sweat trickled down the small of her back, and she fought the impulse to fidget.

Who was this man with his cold eyes and arrogant features? "Please, if you could just speak with Adam Delaney. He knows all about this."

"Unless you find a particularly good medium, talking to him might prove difficult. I'm Matthew Delaney. Adam was my father. He died of a heart attack four days ago. We buried him yesterday.''

Shock rippled through April. To her shame, she realized her grief was not so much for the man who had died, a man she'd hardly known, but rather for the hope he'd represented—the hope of a new start.

''Hi.'' A second man joined Matthew in the doorway. It was easy to tell the two men were related. Both appeared to have been forged in darkness: ebony hair, shadowed gray-blue eyes and thick dark brows that instantly emitted an aura of disapproval. They both towered over her five feet two inches, and this second man was shirtless, exposing a tanned, impossibly broad, muscled chest.

''Go on, Mark,'' Matthew said. ''I'll handle this.''

Mark smiled, and any air of darkness vanished. It was the open smile of a guileless man. ''I'm Mark Delaney,'' he said, and held out his hand.

''I'm April. April Cartwright.'' She allowed him to shake her hand, startled at the unexpected firmness of his grasp. His hand was warm, his palm slightly callused.

''April. That's a pretty name. Like spring.'' He looked eminently pleased with himself for making the connection between her name and the season, and at that moment April suspected the tall, devastatingly handsome cowboy in front of her was mentally challenged.

''Go home, Ms. Cartwright. There's nothing for you here,'' Matthew Delaney said curtly.

''But you don't understand.'' April bit her bottom lip, not quite able to bring herself to beg. What was she going to tell Brian? She'd made so many promises to her son. "We have no home to go to," she finally said.

"You can stay here," Mark said, then turned to Matthew. "She could stay in one of the back cottages. Let her stay, Matthew." He looked back at April and smiled shyly. "I like her."

Matthew stared at Mark, then looked back at April. He raked a hand through his dark hair and frowned. "You can stay for the night. I can't promise anything beyond that."

It wasn't what April needed, and it certainly wasn't what she'd expected, but if she couldn't have the whole loaf, she'd take whatever crumbs were offered. "Thank you," she replied.

At least she and Brian could get a good night's sleep before leaving to go to— To go where? There was nothing to return to. At the moment the sum of her future consisted of a single night in a cottage.

"If you'll give me just a moment, I'll show you where you can spend the night," Matthew said. It was obvious by his closed expression he was not particularly happy with Mark's interference.

"I can show her," Mark replied.

Matthew looked at him dubiously. "You sure?"

Mark nodded. "I can do it."

Matthew hesitated another moment, then looked at April. "Mark will show you where you can stay. One night, that's the best I can offer you. We're not even sure there will be a Delaney Dude Ranch tomorrow."

"Thank you," April replied.

"Don't thank me," Matthew said. "You can thank

Mark.'' Without another word he turned and left the doorway.

Mark stepped out onto the porch, bringing with him the scent of a freshly showered male.

''Maybe we should just go,'' April said. It was obvious Matthew Delaney wasn't pleased with even giving the reprieve of a night. ''Matthew didn't seem too happy.''

''Matthew is my brother, and he's never happy,'' Mark replied. ''It's all right. Come on, I'll show you.'' When she hesitated, again he smiled that wondrously warm smile. ''Come on,'' he repeated.

April followed him from the porch and gestured for her son to join them. Brian bounded from the car, all skinny arms and legs. His face was lit with eagerness.

''Brian, this is Mark. Mark, this is my son, Brian.''

''How do you do, sir?'' Brian said.

Mark grinned widely, as if Brian had told a joke. ''My name isn't sir, it's Mark.''

Brian looked at April, a question in his gaze. April shook her head, indicating to him that they'd talk later.

Mark led them around the huge, rambling ranch house. To the left of the house were the guest quarters, attractive little cottages, which at the moment were empty.

When April had spoken with Adam Delaney a week before, she'd been told that the ranch had two dark months a year, months when they didn't take guests, one month in the spring and one month in the fall. The down time was used for major repairs and cleaning. This was the last two weeks of the spring down time.

In two weeks time, the dude ranch would be jumping with guests, families and newlyweds, young couples and old, all here to enjoy the novelty of the Old West that the resort offered, unless, as Matthew Delaney had indicated, Adam's death was also the demise of the highly reputed dude ranch.

April was intensely conscious of the man next to her. He walked with a loose-hipped gait just shy of a swagger. He was all man yet, in his eyes, in his smile, he appeared rather simple.

As they walked, the midday sun beat down with relentless heat, and thick dust rode a breeze that seemed to spew straight from a blast furnace.

She struggled for small talk, but was too tired, too hot and too disheartened. Besides, she couldn't very well comment on the beauty of their surroundings. There was nothing but barrenness. A land suffering sunstroke. Scrub grass struggled to survive in the blistered red earth, where cacti seemed to be the only vegetation that flourished.

Inferno, Arizona. The tiny town southwest of Tucson, near the Mexican border, was to have been the place for her to start fresh, begin to build something good.

She was in the middle of hell, with no job, no money and an eleven-year-old boy who'd been angry at the world for the past two months.

Behind the big house was another group of outbuildings, these less attractive and smaller than the guest bungalows. "Number three," Mark said, breaking the silence between them. He stepped up on the small porch and thumped the black numeral nailed to the door. ''See, number three.''

Again Brian looked at April, as if sensing something not quite right with the tall, handsome cowboy. ''Thank you, Mark,'' she said.

A pleasant smile curved his lips. ''Welcome,'' he returned, then clapped Brian on the back. ''Come on, let's get your stuff from the car.''

''You don't have to do that,'' April protested. He'd already done enough by convincing his brother to allow them to stay for the night.

''I can do it,'' Mark replied. ''I'm strong.''

Oh, there was no doubt he was strong. His broad chest and thick biceps attested to that fact. He was strong but seemed gentle at the same time.

''Let us guys do it, Mom,'' Brian said.

A lump rose in her throat and she nodded. She watched as Mark and Brian went back to her parked car.

Brian matched his stride to that of Mark's, looking achingly youthful as he struggled to keep up. He'd been so excited about living on a real dude ranch with horses and cows and wide-open spaces.

How was she going to tell him that they were only here for the night? She'd made so many promises to him, certain that finally things were going to go their way for a change.

With a weary sigh she stepped into the small bungalow. It was a cheerless place, furnished with bland, utilitarian furniture. Next to the kitchenette was a narrow, drop-leaf table and two chairs. The living room contained a wall of shelves, a sofa bed and an Early-American coffee table, whose base was shaped like a wagon wheel. In each of the two bedrooms was a double bed and a small chest of drawers.

At least there's a shower, she thought as she went into the bathroom. At the moment a shower sounded divine.

When she heard the sound of footsteps on the porch, she left the bathroom. Mark entered first, carrying two suitcases. Brian followed just behind him with the ice chest that contained the last of the fruit and cheese they'd nibbled on the ride.

"We have to make another trip to get the rest of it," Brian said.

"That's enough for now," April replied. No sense unloading everything from the car when they would only be packing it again tomorrow.

Mark set the suitcases just inside the door, then walked over and turned on the window air conditioner. "You'll fry like bacon if you don't use this."

Brian looked around, then called to his mother, "Which bedroom is going to be mine?"

"You can have the bigger of the two," she replied, dreading the moment she had to tell him it was only for one night.

She smiled once more at Mark. "Thank you again for your help. We'll be fine now."

He reached out and took her hand in his. Instantly warmth seeped up her arm. She held his hand for a moment too long, wanting to convey to him how grateful she was for the reprieve he'd granted them.

When she finally dropped his hand, she was startled to see a flash of…something in his eyes. It was there only a moment, then gone.

"You'll be fine," he agreed. Again he smiled a

sweet, uncomplicated smile. "I'll be back later." With this promise he turned and left them alone.

"He's nice, but something isn't working right," Brian said as he tapped the side of his head.

He'd been more than nice, April thought, and his smile had reached inside her and touched her like none had in a very long time.

Perhaps because it had been such a nonthreatening, gentle smile. No cunning, no shrewdness, nothing but innocent pleasure. The smile of innocence and yet it had warmed her like that of a man's.

She shook her head, dismissing all thoughts of Mark Delaney. She had more important things to think about—like the fact that come morning, they'd be back on the road to nowhere.

As Mark walked toward the stables, he wondered what had prompted him to come to April Cartwright's rescue. Had it been because her hair was the rich-gold of a daisy, or because her dewy, green eyes had radiated the promise of spring—something Inferno, Arizona, didn't normally enjoy?

Or had it simply been because he'd felt her desperation, sensed a disturbing resignation? She'd looked so small, so defenseless when Matthew had told her there was no position available.

Adam had promised her a job, and now Adam was gone. A shaft of pain pierced through Mark as he thought of his father.

He grieved not so much for the man who had died, but for the fact that now he and his father would never be anything more than what they'd been to each other—virtual strangers.

Shoving aside these thoughts, he entered the stable. As always the scent of oiled leather, fresh hay and horseflesh filled him with pleasure and a sense of homecoming.

The horses had always been his family, the stable his home. As he walked down the center of the building, the horses in their stalls on either side greeted him with soft whinnies and welcoming nickers.

He whispered soft words to each animal he passed, pausing to stroke a mane or scratch behind an ear. There was no sound of another human being, and Mark knew the men who worked for the ranch would be on their lunch break.

What had happened to April and Brian Cartwright? No money and no place to go. What kicks had life delivered to them that had landed them here, broke and hopeless?

He couldn't very well ask such questions. He wasn't supposed to be bright enough to understand such things.

Frowning, he reached up and touched the back of his head. In the past three weeks, the wound had nearly healed, although he'd led everyone to believe the assault had left behind inexplicable brain damage.

Although the physical wounds were mending, he was still suffering from a disturbing rage. He was racked by the need to discover who had attacked him with a shovel and who had killed Marietta Lopez.

A vision of Marietta exploded in his mind. Dancing dark eyes and a generous smile, the attractive young woman had been a favorite among both guests and the other workers at the ranch.

But the last time Mark had seen her, she hadn't

been smiling and the light in her eyes hadn't danced. Her eyes had shone with the darkness of secrets. She'd been afraid.

How he wished he had a clue as to her murderer and what secrets she hadn't had the opportunity to share with him. How he wished she'd been as hard-headed as he was, then perhaps the blow from the shovel wouldn't have killed her.

Was it possible he'd seen something in April's eyes that had reminded him of Marietta's that night? The same kind of fear, the same expression of anxiety?

April. Her eyes had been the brightest green he'd ever seen and something in their depths had stirred him—a slight wariness, a vulnerability. The look of a dog that desperately wanted a soft touch, but anticipated a swift kick.

She'd said she'd been hired by his father as social director. The position had opened up when Marietta had been murdered.

If, at the family meeting at dinnertime, his brothers, Matthew and Luke, and his sister, Johnna, decided to abide by the terms of their father's will and work the ranch together for the next year, then they would need a social director.

Of course, it was possible the Delaney siblings would do what they had always done in the past—go their separate ways. The ranch would then be sold and the money go to their aunt Clara. For his sake, as well as for April Cartwright's, he hoped that didn't happen.

He turned at the sound of raucous male laughter and tensed as John Lassiter, the foreman, and several of the cowboys came into view.

"Hey, Mark," Billy Carr called out, a wise-guy smirk on his narrow face. "How's it going?"

Mark forced his smile. "How's what going?" He sighed inwardly with resignation, knowing what was about to follow. Bait the fool. It had become a favorite game among the Neanderthals since Mark's supposed brain damage had become common knowledge.

"Life, my boy." Billy clapped him on the back, at the same time winking at the others. "How's life for a man who is one crayon short of a box?"

"One fry shy of a Happy Meal," Kip Randall chimed in, exposing protruding front teeth as he guffawed with ill-spirited laughter.

"That's enough," John snapped, calling a halt to their fun. "Get to work, both of you." When the two had disappeared in the direction of the barn, John turned and smiled at Mark. "You okay?"

"Sure, I'm okay."

"Don't you pay any attention to them two," John said. "They're morons."

Mark nodded, his grin unchanging. And they would be the first two to be fired when Mark achieved his goals and reclaimed his intelligence, he thought with satisfaction.

"Mark, could you take a look at Diamond? I thought she was limping earlier this morning. You're the only one she'll let get close to her."

"Sure," Mark agreed. "I'll do it now."

Despite his supposed short falls, nobody questioned his proficiency with the horses. From the time he'd been young, he'd had a special gift with the animals. He could play the idiot in all areas of his life except this one, and he wouldn't allow anyone else to tend to the horses.

It took him only a few minutes to check out Diamond, the palomino that had been his father's favorite mount. A stone in the shoe was easily dislodged, giving the horse instant relief.

When he finished, he headed back to the house. Although he had his own cabin on the outreaches of the Delaney property, Matthew had insisted he stay at the house since the murder attempt.

Whenever possible he went to his own place, where he could drop the facade of fool and just be himself for a few precious moments.

He saw nobody when he entered the house. He knew Lucinda would be in the kitchen preparing the evening meal. Matthew was probably in the study, where he'd spent most of the past four days since Adam's death.

Mark went directly to his room in the back of the house. From the vantage point of his window, he could see the cottages where some of the household help lived and where April and her son were spending the night.

For the first time, as he thought of April Cartwright, he almost regretted the role he'd chosen to play. What woman would be interested in a man like the one he pretended to be?

He turned away from the window with a sigh of disgust. The last thing he needed to even consider was getting involved with any woman. Getting involved meant learning about and sharing pieces of yourself— something Mark could not do. At this point in his life he couldn't risk trusting anyone.

He had to find out what Marietta had wanted to tell him that night. She'd implied whatever it was put the entire ranch operation at risk. Whatever it had been had caused her death and Mark's near death.

He couldn't allow anything to distract him from his goals, including a shapely blonde with springtime eyes and an aura of vulnerability. He had to find a murderer. As Marietta warned him, he couldn't trust the sheriff. Nor could he believe Broder's theory that a missing ranch hand had been responsible for the murder.

By the time Mark had showered once again, washing off the scent of the stables, and had changed his clothes, he realized it must be getting close to dinnertime. As he checked his reflection in the bathroom mirror, his stomach clenched with tension.

Family powwows had never been particularly pleasant, and Mark didn't anticipate this one being any different. Although his brothers and sister had rallied around him when he'd been in the hospital, upon his release they'd returned to their separate lives.

Now, with the terms of their father's will, they were forced to deal with one another. They would either learn to work together in order to keep the ranch alive, or they would choose to continue their solitary lives and the ranch would die along with their father.

As Mark went down the stairs to the dining room, he shook his head ruefully. It was rather amazing to him that Adam, in his death, was attempting to make them all what they had never really ever been in his life—a family.

Chapter 2

"I'm not about to give up my law practice to shovel horse dung here." Johnna Delaney glared at Matthew. She had the same bold, dark features as her brothers, and at the moment those features were twisted into a frown. "I can't imagine what father was thinking of when he wrote this will."

The evening meal was finished, and the Delaney siblings had all gathered in the study to discuss the future.

"Well, I'm not exactly champing at the bit to work the ranch," Luke drawled lazily as he poured himself another drink.

Luke, Mark's younger brother, was a sometime musician, a sometime carpenter and an all-the-time hell-raiser. Had it been a hundred years earlier, he probably would have been a gunslinger.

As had been the custom, particularly in the past

three weeks, the conversation swirled around Mark, rather than included him. Nobody asked his opinion, offered him suggestions or spoke directly to him at all.

He was virtually invisible, as he'd felt for most of his life as the middle son sandwiched between the two strong personalities of his older and younger brothers.

"Then we just let it all go?" The muscles in Matthew's jaw tightened visibly. "All Father's hard work and dreams, all the years of planning and struggling, we just let it die with him?" He glared first at Luke, then at Johnna.

Johnna flushed and looked down at the glass of wine she held. "I'm not moving back here, Matthew. This dude ranch was always yours and Mark's and father's dream, not mine."

Walter Tilley cleared his throat. The diminutive lawyer sat in a wing chair near the fireplace. Until this moment he'd been so quiet, Mark had nearly forgotten he was in attendance.

"If I might interject," he said calmly. "Johnna, your father's will does not stipulate that you must live here at the ranch. You can remain in town and still adhere to the conditions outlined by your father."

"I'll listen," Luke said, a wry grin curving his lips. "I don't know about the rest of you, but losing the money the ranch is worth to Aunt Clara doesn't sit much better with me than giving up my time for a year to work the ranch."

Walter smoothed his thin mustache with the tip of a manicured finger as he stepped in to further explain the terms of the will. "Specifically all the will requires is that you keep the ranch running for a year and that you each put in a total of twenty-five hours per week working a specific position. After the year has passed, you're free to keep the ranch running or sell it and split the proceeds.

"Might I suggest you seriously consider adhering to the terms of the will," he went on. "There would be a considerable amount of money coming to each of you should you decide to sell at the end of the year."

"I don't care about the money," Johnna exclaimed irritably, and walked to the window that looked out onto the front of the property. "I hate it here," she said more to herself than to the others.

"This must be a unanimous decision," Walter said. "Either you all agree or the ranch is sold and the proceeds are paid to Clara Delaney."

There was a long, tension-filled silence.

"I have a new friend," Mark said to nobody in particular. He knew his comment was completely inappropriate but in keeping with the path of subterfuge he'd decided to follow.

"That's good, bro." Luke clapped Mark on the back absently. "So, what's the decision here, gang? I've got plans for the night."

Johnna turned from the window and faced her brothers, then looked at Walter. "Tell me again how this works and who is responsible for what."

Mark stifled a sigh, wondering how many more times they would have to go through all this before a final decision was made. One thing was clear: Matthew wasn't willing to let go of the ranch. Was it because he was involved in the illegal activity Marietta had discovered?

"Your father requested I continue as overseer of ranch finances," Walter explained. "Each of you would log in with me concerning your hours worked here. Matthew, your father wished you to continue as manager, overseeing the daily operation of things. Mark would remain in charge of the livestock. Luke would take care of maintenance and repairs, and you'd handle public relations and publicity."

As Walter continued to talk, Mark cast surreptitious glances to his siblings. He'd like to think he knew them well enough to know that none of them would be involved in any nefarious operations on the ranch. But he couldn't.

Sadly, at thirty-three years old, Mark was no closer to knowing his brothers and sister than he'd been at ten.

"Johnna, please." Matthew's voice was tense and Mark knew the price in pride his older brother paid to beg. Was there also desperation there? "We have to come to a decision now. We've got a full slate of guests due to arrive in two weeks. Just give it a try."

Mark looked at his sister. She was beautiful, but any softness she'd possessed had died when she'd miscarried in the sixth month of her pregnancy eight years ago without a man anywhere near her side.

All the pleading in the world wouldn't move Johnna if she didn't want to be moved. She'd become hard. Hard enough to get involved in illegal activity, Mark thought.

She sighed and looked at Luke. It had always been so, that the two youngest, Johnna and Luke, had a closeness that excluded their two elder brothers.

Luke shrugged with his usual devil-may-care grin.

"Why don't we try it for three months, then see how things are going? We can always walk away at that time. What do you say, Mark? We give it a try?"

"Sure," Mark agreed then added, "My new friend's name is April." He smiled at his brothers and sister as if he didn't feel the raw emotion, the heightened tension in the air. If only he could trust his family enough to let go of the fool's role, he thought. But he couldn't forget Marietta's words of warning.

"April?" Luke raised an eyebrow in Matthew's direction.

Matthew waved his hand in dismissal. "I'll explain later," he said, his gaze focused intently on Johnna.

"All right," she said to Matthew, her features taut with irritation. "I'll give it a try. Not for father's sake, but because I know how important the ranch is to you and Mark."

"Then it's settled," Walter said as he stood. "I'll be in touch with each of you later this week to work out the details."

Mark stood, grateful the matter had been decided and eager to escape. Throughout dinner and during the entire discussion about the ranch, all he'd been able to think about was April and Brian and the cooler of food.

He'd seen the contents of the cooler when Brian had nearly upended it when he'd grabbed it from the back seat of their car. It had been a scant amount of fruit, several hunks of cheese and a couple cans of soda.

As he'd eaten his dinner of roast and potatoes, fresh corn and homemade bread, he'd thought of them din-

ing on their pitiful fare and had decided a care basket
was in order.

Matthew walked the others to the front door, and
Mark made his escape into the kitchen. Lucinda, the
woman who'd been cooking for the Delaney family
for as long as Mark could remember, had already left
for the night. The enormous kitchen was spotless, but
Mark knew there were always plenty of leftovers in
the refrigerator.

He grabbed a basket from the pantry, then checked
out the contents of the large, stainless steel refrigerator. Spying several pieces of fried chicken from the
night before, he wrapped them in foil and put them
into a basket. He added a container of potato salad, a
small tub of baked beans and bread and butter.

Then, thinking of the boy, he wrapped up half of
the chocolate cake Lucinda had baked that day and
added it to the basket.

He left by the back door, catching his breath as he
stepped from the cool of the house into the heat of
the evening. It was mid-May, but already the tem-
peratures were consistently hitting the century mark.

As he walked toward the cottages, once again his
thoughts went to the role he'd chosen to play. Initially
he'd just wanted to buy himself some time, to gain
enough distance from that night with Marietta in order
to make sense of it all.

As soon as he'd started the pretense, he'd noticed
something interesting. People talked in front of him
as if he wasn't present. It was an odd phenomenon,
one he had recognized years before when they'd had
a Down's syndrome man working for them. Mark had
noticed how people spoke in front of the man about

things they would never confide to anyone else, as if confident he would never repeat, or understand, what they were saying.

And that was exactly what Mark was counting on now. Already he'd noticed the ranch hands spoke more freely in front of him than they ever had in the past. And in that freedom, Mark hoped to glean clues about Marietta's murder and whatever it was she had believed threatened the very existence of the ranch.

He shoved these thoughts aside as he reached cottage number three. He was surprised as an eager anticipation surged through him.

Now that they had decided to keep the ranch running for at least three months, April and Brian would be able to stay. Somehow, he'd make sure of it. He didn't stop to analyze why it was important to him that they remain at the ranch. It was enough that she reminded him of spring.

He shifted the basket from one hand to the other, then knocked on the door.

She answered almost immediately, and it was obvious she had recently stepped out of a shower. Her hair was curly and damp and she smelled of soap and shampoo. She was clad in a mint-colored, sleeveless shift that skimmed her slenderness and stopped just above her knees.

"Mark." Her eyes widened as she saw him.

"I brought a surprise," he said, and held up the basket.

"A surprise?" A tiny wrinkle furrowed her brow as she gazed first at him, then at the basket. "Please come in." She stepped aside to allow him entry, then

closed the door behind her to stop the flow of heat
into the air-conditioned room.

A small suitcase was open on the sofa, revealing
pastel-colored lacy things, and the sight of those feminine items caused a flutter of heat to sweep through
Mark.

He set the basket on the table, wondering what it
was about this particular woman that affected him on
a level that nobody else had for a very long time.

He'd been invulnerable, untouchable both physically and mentally when it came to women since Rachel's defection three years ago.

"What's all this?" she asked, peering into the basket.

"Dinner."

Her eyes appeared to grow impossibly luminous.
"Oh," she said softly. "Mark, you shouldn't have
done this."

"Why not? It's good food." He rocked back on
his heels and shoved his hands in his pockets.

She laughed, a musical sound that was at once arresting. "I'm sure it's good food."

"Then eat," Mark replied. He pulled his hands
from his pocket and began to unload the items from
the basket. "Where's your boy?" he asked when he'd
finished.

She pointed toward the closed bedroom door.
"He's angry."

"Why?" Mark went to the cabinet and pulled out
two plates and set them on the table.

Again her brow crinkled with a frown, and he could
tell she was trying to determine whether to tell him.
"I had promised Brian we were going to stay here,

that I was going to have a job here. Now he's angry because there's no job and we'll be leaving in the morning.''

"You're going to stay," Mark replied confidently. He walked over to the bedroom door and rapped on it, then smiled at April. "We had a family meeting. The ranch is going to stay open and you will have a job."

"But your father hired me, and now he's gone. Perhaps your brother will want to interview—"

"You have the job," Mark interrupted her, then knocked once again on the door. "Brian, come out."

The door opened and Brian stepped out, a mulish expression on his face. "What?" he said with more than a touch of belligerence.

"Come and eat," Mark said.

"I'm not hungry," Brian said, but he moved closer to the table, and his eyes widened at the sight of the chocolate cake. "Well, maybe I could eat just a little," he said and slid into one of the chairs at the table.

"Go on," Mark urged April into the other chair, then he shoved the suitcase over and sank onto the sofa.

"This was so incredibly kind of you," April said, her gaze so warm on him, he could feel the heat clear down to his toes.

He nodded and fell silent, afraid of saying too much, not wanting to expose himself, yet wishing to hell he could reveal himself to her.

He wanted to know where she and Brian were from, how Adam had come to hire her, what forces had driven her here. He wanted to know if her skin was as soft as it looked, if it would be warm and inviting beneath his touch.

And he wanted to know why her beautiful, thick-lashed eyes emitted such fragility. He had a feeling keeping up his act with her was going to be the most difficult thing he'd ever done.

April ate self-consciously, unsure what to make of the man who sat on the sofa. His kindness in bringing them dinner had nearly undone her, and it was only with enormous effort that she hadn't cried.

She only picked at the food on her plate, finding Mark Delaney far more interesting than chicken and beans. He was a fascinating dichotomy, his face an arresting contrast of darkness and light.

With his strong, bold features, short black hair and thick dark brows over dark gray-blue eyes, he emitted an aura of hard arrogance, of cool confidence that was instantly dispelled by the sweet gentleness of his smile.

It was such a refreshing change from the men in her past, the two men who had betrayed her on every level possible. She shoved this thought aside, refusing to drown in past regrets. She also shoved aside her plate and left the table.

She moved the suitcase to the floor and joined Mark on the sofa. "I want to thank you again, Mark, for your thoughtfulness," she said.

He shrugged and smiled. "I'd be glad to get the rest of your stuff from the car. You're staying— I mean, if you want to stay."

"We can stay?" Brian jumped up from the table and looked at Mark hopefully. "Really and truly?"

"Cross my heart and hope to die," Mark replied solemnly. "You like horses?"

"Well, sure," Brian replied. "But I don't know much about them. But I could learn," he hurriedly added. "Maybe you could hire me to help in the stables. You don't have to pay me a lot, just some so I can help Mom."

His eagerness caused an ache in April's heart. Her little boy, trying so hard to be a man. He should be spending his summer vacation playing with friends, listening to music and conquering video games. Instead he was worrying about getting a job and helping take care of living expenses. How had their world gotten so topsy-turvy?

"Brian, let's take things one step at a time," April warned. As much as she'd love to take this handsome cowboy at his word, she had a feeling his word probably didn't carry much weight and it was Matthew Delaney who would make the decision about whether they remained here.

"Brian, if you're finished eating, it's time for a shower," April said.

He started to balk. April knew the idea of a shower to her son was as abhorrent as kissing a girl. But, having just asked Mark about a job, Brian apparently thought a temper tantrum might not be in his best interest. He nodded and disappeared into the bathroom.

"Where's his dad?" Mark asked.

"Gone." The word fell flatly from her.

"Like mine."

She nodded, although it wasn't quite the same. Derrick wasn't dead. He was someplace alive and kick-

ing, never staying in one place long enough for creditors to find him. "You mentioned a family meeting.
Besides Matthew do you have other brothers and sis-
ters?"

Mark nodded. "Luke. He's a mess. That's what
Matthew says."

April laughed, finding his candor refreshing. "Matthew, Mark and Luke," she said.

"And Johnna, my sister."

"Your father was a religious man, I take it."

"My aunt Clara says he was a religious man only
on Sundays." Mark grinned as she laughed once
more. "You sound nice when you laugh."

"Thank you." April was surprised to feel a warm
blush creep over her features. She stood, vaguely un-
comfortable with the feelings he evoked in her…feel-
ings she'd believed long dead.

"I'll put the leftovers in the basket, and you can
take them back with you," she said, busying herself
with clearing the table.

"Just keep them." He joined her near the table.
"You didn't have a piece of cake."

"No," she agreed.

"You don't like chocolate?" He gazed at her with
studied intensity and April found her breath catching
in her chest. He looked at her with the eyes of a man
who knew what he wanted…and might just want her.

She broke the gaze, heat swirling inside her. "I
love chocolate."

"Good, then let's have a piece of cake." His big
capable hand swallowed hers as he grabbed it and
pulled her into a chair at the table. He released her

hand and gestured toward the cake in the center of the table.

Suddenly a piece of cake sounded good.

"Lucinda is the best baker in the entire world," he said as she cut them each a piece.

"Lucinda?"

"She's our cook. She's sort of taken care of us since we were all little." He took a bite of his cake. "Where did you live before you came here?"

She mentally shifted gears in order to keep up with his ever-changing topics of conversation. "We're from Tulsa, Oklahoma."

"Did you know my father?" he asked.

"No, I'm sorry, I didn't. Although my father knew him." April shoved the last of her cake aside; as always, thoughts of her father filled her with incredible ambiguity.

She'd loved her father with all her heart, but the man she'd always believed would protect her and love her had ultimately betrayed her as badly as her husband had.

"I've made you sad." Mark's gentle voice pulled her from her thoughts, and she looked at him, surprised by his sharp sensitivity and the empathy that radiated from his eyes.

"No," she protested. "You haven't made me sad." She sighed. "Lately life has made me sad."

"How come?" His big, broad hand moved to cover hers, its warmth as intense as the midday Inferno sun. Again April felt as if she couldn't get enough air, as if somehow his touch displaced the oxygen in the room.

She wanted to tell him never mind, but his soft

gaze held hers, and a slight pressure from his hand over hers encouraged the words to fall from her.

As nice as his hand felt covering hers, she pulled hers away and stood. Someplace in the back of her mind, she knew it was crazy to tell this man, this stranger, her life story.

Maybe the fact that she figured he probably wouldn't understand all of it and couldn't really judge her, made it seem overwhelmingly easy to consider baring her soul.

But that didn't explain why his simple touch affected her so. "Let's just say I have a terrible habit of trusting the wrong people," she finally said, deciding baring one's soul was far overrated.

At that moment, before Mark could make any reply, Brian came out of the bathroom clad in his usual sleeping attire, an oversize T-shirt and a pair of athletic shorts. "Hey, you guys had cake without me," he protested.

"You can have yours now," April replied.

Brian sat down in the chair where April had been and gazed at Mark eagerly. "Do you know how to ride buckin' broncos and throw a lasso?"

Mark grinned, a slow, lazy expression that stirred fire in April's veins. Despite his apparent slightly diminished mental capacity, she found him disturbingly attractive. There was something very sexy in his smile and a knowing glint that sparked in the depths of his eyes. "Sure," he replied.

"Could you teach me how to ride broncos and throw a lasso?" Brian asked.

"Maybe," Mark said, then frowned. "Although we

ought to start off with the rope instead of riding a bronco.''

April smiled at him. ''I think that's definitely wise.''

''It's wise? Good.'' Mark grinned, as if extremely satisfied with himself.

April's heart constricted with compassion. She wondered if Mark had been born slow, or if he'd had an accident as a child.

Her compassion had nothing to do with pity. It was difficult to pity a man who, despite any mental imperfections, exuded such quiet strength, who seemed to fit so well in his own skin and who radiated peace and happiness despite any depth of intelligence he might be lacking. It was impossible to pity a man who looked sexy enough to make her knees weaken.

''Tell me about the horses,'' Brian asked, leaning forward eagerly.

As Mark talked about the horses and his responsibilities with them, April leaned against the refrigerator, entranced by the transformation that seemed to occur in him.

He began haltingly, his words and descriptions coming as if through sheer, intense concentration alone. But it was obvious the topic of conversation was one he felt comfortable with, confident about, and that confidence shone from his eyes, filling them with a compelling animation and life that had been heretofore missing.

A knock on the door interrupted the conversation. April opened it to see Matthew Delaney.

''Good evening,'' he greeted her, his gaze instantly

going beyond her to Brian and Mark at the table. "Mark, I wondered where you'd gone to."

"I'm right here," Mark replied.

"Yes, I can see that now." Matthew focused his attention back on April. "It appears that we'll be keeping the ranch open for the time being, so if you're still interested in the position of social director, it's yours."

April's heart soared. "Yes...oh, yes, I want the job."

Matthew nodded, his stern features not relaxing at all. "If you'll come to the house tomorrow around noon, we'll go over the terms of your employment and I'll give you all the files from the previous social director."

"Thank you so much. I promise you won't be sorry," she exclaimed.

Again he nodded as his gaze sought his brother. "Mark, it's getting late. You need to come back to the house now."

Mark stood and clapped Brian on the back. "If you want to start work, be at the stables at seven in the morning."

"Cool!" Brian exclaimed. "I'll be there."

Mark stepped out onto the porch with his brother, then smiled at April, that warm smile that forged a path straight to her heart. "I'll see you tomorrow, April."

She nodded. "Good night, Mark."

She remained on the porch and watched the two brothers walking away. They were like bookends, equal in height and breadth of shoulder, but she found nothing particularly pleasing or attractive about Matthew Delaney.

With a sigh she turned and went back into the small cottage. Minutes later she tucked Brian into bed. It had been a long day, most of it spent in the confines of the car, and although it was relatively early, his eyelids drooped with sleepiness.

"Don't forget to wake me up early," Brian said. "I've got to be in the stables by seven."

"Don't worry, I'll get you up in time," she assured him. She stroked a strand of his dark hair off his forehead, as always marveling how much the child looked like his father. It was as if Brian had been cloned from Derrick's rib and had nothing of her physical characteristics.

There were times in the dark of night when April's biggest fear was that her son would grow up to be just like Derrick—a weak man without character, without good values. The only two men who had been a part of Brian's life, who had any profound influence, had been sad, weak imitations of men.

"Mom? Something's wrong with Mark, isn't it?" Brian eyed her sleepily.

"Yes, honey. I think maybe something is wrong. I think maybe he's just a little slow."

"But he's not stupid," Brian replied.

"No, I don't think he's stupid."

"It's okay if I like him, isn't it?"

April smiled at her son. "Yes, it's okay that you like him."

"Good." Brian closed his eyes and within moments was fast asleep.

April remained seated on the edge of the bed,

watching her son sleep. For the past two months, since her own father's death, Brian had been unruly, difficult and possessing a simmering anger that had April at her wit's end. But from the moment he'd learned they were staying here, and while he'd been interacting with Mark, he'd transformed back to the child of her heart, with smiles and good humor.

April left the bedroom and closed the door behind her, her thoughts filled with Mark Delaney. Certainly April wasn't looking for an intimate relationship with any man, but friendship would be nice, especially for Brian's sake.

As she went into her own bedroom, she realized this was the first time in as long as she could remember that thoughts of tomorrow didn't bring despair, but rather brought hope.

Chapter 3

It was just before ten when April walked toward the stables in search of Brian. She needed to go into the small town of Inferno and pick up some groceries, since it appeared they were going to stay.

She'd slept better than she had since her father's death. No dreams had haunted her, no worries had kept sleep at bay. She'd awakened at dawn, feeling for the first time in a long time that she was ready to take on her future.

Already the sun was intense, heating her shoulders and the back of her neck where she'd pulled her hair into a ponytail and exposed pale, untanned skin. She tried to imagine what the heat would be like in July or August, but found it impossible to envision.

Brian wasn't in the stables, so April decided to try the barn. The structure rose before her but there was no sign of Brian anywhere around the outside. She opened the large, double door and stepped into the interior, where she was instantly greeted by the scent of dust, grain, hay and leather.

Although she didn't immediately see Brian, she heard the murmur of voices in the distance. She followed the voices to a small tack room where Brian and Mark were working side by side. They had their backs to her, and for a moment she merely watched, not alerting them to her presence.

Brian was oiling a saddle, and Mark was watching him. "Make sure you're getting it into all the cracks," Mark said.

"Like this?" Brian asked.

Mark watched a moment. "Perfect," he replied, then patted Brian's back. "You're doing a great job." Brian appeared to grow taller beneath Mark's praise.

April's heart expanded with love for her son and gratitude for the man who was taking time with him. Brian had such a hunger inside him, a hunger for male companionship, a hunger that radiated from his eyes and made April feel helplessly inadequate.

"Hi," she said.

They both spun around at the sound of April's voice.

"Hi, Mom." Brian's smile was huge, and April tried to remember when she'd seen him look so genuinely happy. It had been a long time...too long. Especially since his grandfather's death, Brian had been a powder keg of emotions, sometimes exploding in a burst of anger or simply simmering in sullen silence. It was good to see his eyes sparkling with pleasure for a change.

"Hi, April." Mark swept his hat off his head.

"We're just oiling down some tack." His smile warmed her as effectively as the sun outside. Why was she so drawn to this man, she wondered.

She walked over and placed a hand on Brian's shoulder. "I was wondering if I could borrow this cowboy for an hour or so. I've got to get into town and get some supplies."

"Okay," Mark agreed easily. He set his hat on a workbench and picked up a towel and wiped his hands. "Mind if I join you?"

April looked at him in surprise, unsure how to reply. "I...well, sure...if it's all right."

"All right?" He gazed at her blankly.

"All right with your brother." April felt the warmth of a blush steal over her cheeks. It seemed odd telling a grown man he'd better check with his brother before going into town. But she knew Mark was no ordinary grown man.

"It's all right," he assured her. He handed Brian the towel.

"Then, let's go," Brian said enthusiastically.

Although April was not particularly comforted by Mark's reassurance that it would be fine if he went along, she didn't know how to gracefully ask him to check with his older brother.

She didn't know many cowboys, but she suspected they were a breed of men with a tall share of pride. The last thing she wanted to do was wound Mark's pride. "Okay, let's go."

As they walked from the barn to the car, April shot him a surreptitious glance. He looked like a poster image for the Old West with his hat riding low on his forehead and shadowing his features and his worn jeans hugging the length of his long legs.

April tore her gaze from the handsome cowboy and instead focused on her son, who was chattering about all the things he'd learned that morning. "Did you know a horse will eat oats and grain until it gets sick? Mark says they don't have sense enough to stop once they start."

April smiled. "I thought only eleven-year-old boys did that."

"Ah, Mom," Brian said with a giggle. He got into the back seat, leaving the front passenger seat for Mark.

Moments later April was driving toward the small town of Inferno, trying to ignore the pleasant scent that wafted from the man next to her. He smelled like the sun, mingled with minty soap and the whisper of an earthy cologne.

They rode in silence for a few minutes, April searching for some topic of pleasant conversation.

"Mom, why don't you turn on the radio?" Brian asked, as if the silence bothered him.

"Won't do you much good," Mark replied. "Inferno only picks up one signal, and it's a local channel owned by old man Butterfield."

"What kind of music do they play?" Brian asked.

"Not much. About the only time the station has music is when Butterfield lets his wife or his daughter sing." A charming, slightly mischievous smile lit Mark's features. "They're nice people, but when they sing, one sounds like a cow giving birth and the other sounds like a baby calf bawling for its mama."

April laughed, and Brian giggled. "I think maybe we'll skip the radio," April said.

"Besides, if the radio is playing, it's harder to talk," Mark observed.

"What do you want to talk about?" Brian asked. He leaned forward, half hanging over the front seat.

"Why don't we talk about car safety?" April suggested. "Sit back and buckle up."

"Ah, Mom, I'm not a baby," Brian protested.

"A cowboy never rides in a car without buckling in," Mark replied sternly.

To April's astonishment Brian sat back and buckled up. April flashed Mark a grateful smile. "Tell me more about cowboys," Brian said eagerly.

Mark turned slightly in his seat, so he was facing April and able to gaze at Brian in the back. He flashed an easy grin. "What do you want to know about them?"

"I want to know everything about them, 'cause I want to be one," Brian exclaimed fervently.

"Cowboys are men who live by a code of honor."

"A code of honor?" Brian's voice held a touch of awe. "What's that mean?"

"It means you mind your mama, you take care of your horse and you never lose your hat."

"I don't even have a hat," Brian said mournfully.

"We'll get you one after payday, Brian," April promised, grateful he'd mentioned the lack of a hat and not the omission of a horse in his life. She could probably swing a cowboy hat out of her first paycheck, but a horse would be impossible.

Within minutes they'd arrived in the small town of Inferno. Built on a square, the little town didn't appear to even try to compete with the impressive court-house at its center. With its wide concrete walkway and four stories of steel and glass, the courthouse looked as incongruous as a magnolia blooming in the middle of the sand.

The rest of the buildings that comprised the town of Inferno were one-story, earth-tone adobe and stucco that gave the impression of longevity and a peaceful coexistence with the desert that surrounded them.

"You can park there." Mark pointed to an empty space in front of a grocery store.

April pulled into the parking space and shut off the engine. "What a charming little town," she said as the three of them got out of the car.

"Come on. Before you buy groceries, I'll show you all my favorite stores," Mark said as he clapped his hat back on top of his head.

As the three of them started down the sidewalk, April looked around with interest. Would this little town eventually feel like home? Could she and Brian find happiness here?

"There's the diner," Mark said, pointing a finger at the storefront with two potted cacti like sentries guarding the door. "They have good apple pie, but don't eat the meat loaf surprise. It's awful."

April laughed. "Meat loaf isn't particularly a favorite of mine, anyway."

She was overly conscious of his nearness, of the scent of him wrapping around her as he walked close enough that she could feel the heat from his body.

"Wow, look!" Brian pointed to a store up ahead,

where the window display consisted of a half-dozen ornate saddles and matching bridles.

"That's the tack shop and next to it is the post office," Mark said.

As he pointed out various places of interest, it was easy for April to forget that he was mentally impaired. He exuded an enthusiasm that was contagious and a candor that was refreshing.

He'd be easy to spend time with, she thought. A good companion who held no threat either emotionally or financially. A friend. She couldn't remember the last time she'd had a friend, and the concept of Mark filling that space in her life warmed her. Perhaps warmed her a tad too much, she thought ruefully.

They stopped when they had gone completely around the square and were back to where April's car was parked.

"I've got stuff to do at some other stores," Mark said. "I'll just meet you back here in a few minutes."

April watched helplessly as he ambled down the sidewalk away from her and Brian. He walked with a masculine grace and for a moment April was completely engrossed in watching the slight sway of his slender hips and the awesome width of his shoulders.

She hoped she hadn't made a mistake in letting him go off on his own. She'd hate to have to go back to the ranch and tell Matthew Delaney that she'd lost his brother.

"Mom?" Brian stared at her impatiently. "Are we going food shopping or what?"

"Yes, we're going food shopping," she said. As she and Brian entered the small grocery store, she shoved her concerns about Mark aside. She had more important concerns—like how to buy the maximum amount of food with a minimum amount of cash.

Mark had discovered that an eleven-year-old boy could be a veritable font of information. Through Brian's early-morning chatter, Mark had learned that April was almost thirty years old, her favorite color was turquoise and sometimes at night she cried when she thought Brian couldn't hear her.

When Rachel had left Mark three years ago and married Samuel Rogers from the ranch nearest the Delaney place, Mark had sworn that he'd never get involved with any woman again.

Rachel had taken his heart, then twisted and mashed it when she'd told him she'd never believed any of the Delaney men would make good husbands or fathers. A month before their wedding date, she'd broken off the relationship and had left Mark bloody and defeated in the arena of romance.

Deep down he knew Rachel had been right in her assessment of him. None of the Delaney men was a good husband or father prospect. Even Johnna hadn't managed to find a relationship that worked for her.

When she'd been eighteen, she'd dated the bad boy of town, Jerrod McCain, but Jerrod had disappeared from her life before her miscarriage, and as far as Mark knew, Johnna had never allowed anyone close to her again.

Matthew had always been too obsessed with the ranch to sustain any relationships, and Luke played at love, enjoying his image as a wild, untamed rake.

The Delaneys were definitely stunted in their ability to maintain any kind of relationship with the opposite sex. Unsurprising, considering they didn't even have good relationships with each other.

No, Mark didn't want a romance with April. He recognized his own inability, the inadequacies in himself that made him a bad candidate for romance. But that didn't mean his fingers didn't itch to touch the gold of April's hair, and he had to confess the scent of her stirred him like no woman had in a very long time.

He walked into the Western clothing store, the small cowbell over the door announcing to the owner that somebody had entered the premises.

"Mark," John Shaffer, the owner of Western Wear, greeted him with a friendly smile and an outstretched hand. His grizzled brow wrinkled in concern as he pumped Mark's hand. "How you feeling? I haven't seen you since your accident."

"I'm okay."

John's hand was warm around Mark's. "I was sorry to hear about your father. He was a good man, Mark."

Mark nodded, surprised that the kind words about his father brought a lump to his throat. "Matthew says I need some new jeans." Mark forced himself to smile the empty expression that he'd perfected over the past several weeks.

John released his hand. "Oh, sure. We can get you set up with a new pair of jeans."

Mark didn't miss the look of pity that flashed momentarily across John's features. Pity. That was the worst part of his subterfuge. The pity he saw on good people's faces, and the smirking derision he saw on not-so-good people's faces.

At least he had yet to see pity on April's face. He'd seen curiosity, bewilderment and interest, but thankfully not pity.

It took only minutes for Mark to get the jeans and charge them to the Delaney account. As he was leaving the store, his attention was captured by the hat display. The wall section held hats of various sizes and styles, including one just like Mark's, only sized to fit a boy's head.

It's not my job to buy that boy a hat, Mark told himself as he moved closer to the display. That kid is nothing to me but a part-time helper in the stables.

He already regretted the impulse that had prompted him to be friendly to April and Brian. He had no time for any kind of relationships, and Rachel had made it quite clear he wasn't very good at them. He needed to back away from April and her son. He was pretending to be something he was not, and there was no guarantee they were going to manage to keep the ranch, no guarantee that April would be around for long.

Despite his internal protests to the contrary, he walked out of the store with both the jeans and the hat. In the distance he saw April and Brian exiting the grocery store, a cart laden with bags in front of them.

Perfect timing, he thought as he hurried toward them. When he reached them, April had opened the trunk and was beginning to unload the bags.

"Here, I'll do that." He threw his packages into

one corner of the trunk, then began to unload the shopping cart.

"You should see all the good stuff Mom bought," Brian said, dancing around Mark like a young colt with too much energy. "She bought frozen pizzas and cookies and chips."

"Hmm, sounds good," Mark said.

"And she bought chopped meat and said I could make hamburgers one night. Maybe you could eat dinner with us and taste my specialty burgers." The boy's need was in his eyes, the need to connect, and it was fierce in its hunger.

"Maybe," Mark replied without commitment, realizing he definitely needed to put some distance between him and them. Brian's hunger was too great, and Mark definitely wasn't the man to fulfill the young boy's needs. Whatever Brian was looking for in his life, whatever April might be seeking, Mark wasn't the answer and never would be.

"Mark Delaney!"

The familiar feminine voice worked like cat claws on a blackboard, shooting irritation straight up his spine. He straightened from the trunk and eyed the attractive red-haired woman bearing down on them.

Molly Weiser. Mark stifled a groan. Of all the people in this world, there were two Mark hated coming face-to-face with—the first was Molly, followed closely by the devil himself.

"Mark, darling."

Before he could successfully weave and dodge, he found himself embraced in a cloud of honeysuckle perfume, large silicon breasts pressed firmly against his chest.

"Molly..." He pulled her away from him and pointed to April. "This is my friend April and her son, Brian."

"Hi, I'm April Cartwright. I'm working for the Delaneys," April said.

"Indeed." Molly's eyes narrowed into suspicious slits. She looked to Mark and back to April. "And from all appearances, you're a fast worker."

April's friendly smile faltered, and Mark wanted to throttle Molly, who turned back to Mark and grabbed his hand. "Darling, I've been wanting to see you since all the trouble, but that dreadful older brother of yours is quite off-putting. I've heard some stories that have had me worried sick about you."

"I'm fine." Mark pulled his hand from hers and grinned like a loony fool. "How are you?"

Molly's brow wrinkled with concern, and he could see the wheels turning in her head. He knew what stories she'd probably heard—that he was addle brained—and he also knew she was weighing her options.

Molly was determined to marry a Delaney. She'd initially set her sights on Matthew, but when he refused to respond to her advances, she'd honed in on Mark. She'd been pursuing him for months. Now Mark was certain she was trying to decide if half a Delaney might not be just as good as a whole Delaney.

"We have to go," he said to nobody in particular, just feeling the need to escape Molly's cloying presence.

"I'll call you, Mark," Molly said. To Mark's ears

it sounded more threat than promise. "You owe me a dinner date."

Mark loaded the last bag into the trunk and slammed the lid. As Molly wiggled her fingers good-bye, Mark, April and Brian got into the car.

For a long moment nobody spoke. April pulled out of the parking space and headed the car back toward the ranch.

Brian broke the silence. "She had the biggest ones I've ever seen."

"Brian!" April exclaimed in protest, although Mark thought he saw a glimmer of laughter in her big green eyes.

"She bought them," Mark replied. "She went to Tucson on vacation and came back three weeks later with big ones."

"Wow," Brian exclaimed as if the notion of women buying breasts was difficult to wrap his mind around. To tell the truth, it had always been difficult for Mark to understand.

"She should have bought a T-shirt or an ashtray instead," Mark observed.

A giggle escaped April, the sound wonderfully feminine and appealing. "When I was little and we went on vacation, I collected bells."

"I don't have any collections 'cause I've never been anywhere," Brian put in mournfully.

"You're young. You've got plenty of time for collections," Mark replied. He noticed April looking at him curiously and realized he'd been talking far too much.

As they approached the ranch, Mark drew into himself, his thoughts turning to Marietta and what information she might have had that had gotten her killed. Something was amiss at the Delaney Dude Ranch, but Mark had yet to discover exactly what it was. Every day that passed without answers only managed to feed his frustration.

The investigation into Marietta's death and Mark's injuries had been desultory at best by Sheriff Broder, who'd decided it was a crime of jealous rage perpetrated by a ranch hand who had subsequently disappeared.

Mark hadn't told the sheriff what Marietta had shared with him. Her warning that it was possible the sheriff might be involved kept him mute where the specifics were concerned.

In two weeks the ranch would be jumping with guests, making his search for Marietta's killer more complicated. And still he had nothing to go on concerning what activity Marietta had been talking about. He was beginning to wonder if his act was all for nothing.

"So, Mark, what are we going to do when we get back to the ranch?" Brian's voice broke through Mark's thoughts, and again Mark felt the boy's hunger. "Maybe you could teach me to lasso?"

"Can't," Mark replied. "I have stuff to do this afternoon. You're on your own for the rest of the day."

He tried not to allow the boy's disappointment to touch him. He had his own problems to deal with. He absolutely, positively refused to get caught up in April and Brian Cartwright.

"Brian, you can't be bothering Mark all the time,"

April told her son gently. "I'm sure he has more important things to do than teach you to throw a rope."

"Maybe tomorrow," Mark said, hating the fact that despite his intentions, something in the boy's eyes got to him.

"Great," Brian agreed eagerly.

When they arrived at the cottage, April opened the trunk and handed Mark his packages. "Thanks, Mark, for the town tour and all your help."

He nodded and pulled the hat from his bag. "Brian." He tossed the boy the black hat.

Brian caught it with both hands, his eyes widening as he realized what he held. "Wow!" he exclaimed. "A hat just like yours." In three long strides, he reached Mark and wrapped his arms awkwardly around Mark's waist.

"Thanks, Mark." Brian stepped away from him, his cheeks pinkened as if his display of affection had embarrassed him.

Mark turned to walk away, trying to ignore the sunburst of warmth in the pit of his stomach.

"Mark."

He paused and turned back to April. "Yeah?"

"Thank you." He was rewarded by a smile from her that warmed him down to his toes and twisted something deep in his gut.

He suddenly realized he had to be careful. For some reason this woman and her son had the potential of touching him where he'd sworn he would never be touched again.

Chapter 4

As April made her way from her cottage to the main house for her noon appointment with Matthew Delaney, her heart still retained the warmth evoked by Mark's generosity.

It had been a very long time since any man had shown April any act of kindness or benevolence. Mark's gift of the hat to Brian, his gift of easy smiles and camaraderie to April, made her almost believe there were good men out there.

She'd almost forgotten that there were men who could be trusted, men who would never dream of taking advantage of a woman, men who didn't know how to be dishonest or deceitful.

She thought of the red-haired woman they'd met in town. Molly something. She was extremely pretty but had a predatory hardness in her eyes when she'd gazed at Mark. The woman had implied a relationship with him, but had mentioned trouble.

What trouble? Perhaps she'd been talking about the death of Adam Delaney?

April had been oddly disappointed to realize Mark might have a relationship with the woman. The look in Molly's eyes had made a protective streak surge up inside April where Mark was concerned.

She wasn't sure where that feeling came from or, in truth, if it was really protectiveness or an odd pang of jealousy.

She certainly wasn't looking for a relationship with any man and she had no idea of the extent of Mark's mental disability. But whatever the disability, it certainly didn't steal away from his attractiveness as a vital, sexy man.

She couldn't help the way the warmth of his smile shot electric currents through her, how the strength in the rippling muscles and width of his shoulders made her want to melt into his embrace.

Dismissing thoughts of Mark, she stepped up on the porch of the main house and knocked on the door. Matthew answered, his stern features forbidding as he ushered her into an office off the entryway.

He stepped behind a large, wooden desk and gestured her to the chair in front of him. She eased down, wondering how two brothers could look so much alike yet be so different. Mark was warmth and laughter, but Matthew Delaney appeared cold and stern.

"Since we last spoke I found the letter from you to my father, and a copy of his letter to you detailing the terms of your employment," Matthew said as he sat behind the desk. "I assume those terms are still agreeable?"

"Yes."

"As I said last night, I can't make any long-term promises to you concerning employment." His eyes darkened. "I have no idea what the future holds for the Delaney Dude Ranch. However, should we have to breach the contract, you will receive the severance pay detailed in my father's letter."

April nodded and sighed inwardly with relief. "I'll work for you as long as you need me." She'd take whatever she could get in an attempt to get back on her feet financially.

He nodded and pulled a large manila folder from a drawer. "Here is the file of the former social director. She kept quite extensive notes and had many plans in the works. We open to a full crowd in two weeks. I'll expect a detailed, workable plan from you in a week." He handed her the thick file.

"The most important thing for you to remember is that it's your job to see that every person who comes here is accommodated with fun things to do. You'll need to set up activities for children, young couples and older people."

April nodded, undaunted by the task ahead of her. She'd done much the same kind of work at the hotel where she'd worked previously. He returned her nod, and she realized it was a dismissal. She stood and started for the door.

"Ms. Cartwright?"

She paused in the doorway and turned back to him.

"Stay away from my brother."

"Excuse me?" She frowned, wondering if she hadn't heard him correctly.

"Stay away from Mark." Matthew eyed her coldly. "I understand from your letter to my father that you've been through some bad times. It would be natural for you to see Mark as the answer to your financial problems. My brother is vulnerable and he has obviously taken a liking to you, but I won't have him toyed with or hurt.''

''I have no intention of doing either,'' April replied with a touch of coolness to her own voice.

''See that you don't.'' He broke his gaze with her and focused on the paperwork on his desk. Again April realized she'd been dismissed.

''Pompous ass,'' April muttered beneath her breath as she headed for the front door. Imagine him even thinking that somehow she was setting Mark up, that she'd assessed him as weak and wealthy and might try to take advantage of that fact.

April gripped the folder more tightly against her chest, indignation sweeping through her. As if she could ever do to somebody else what had been done to her.

She swung open the door and smacked into a person coming in. ''Oh...sorry,'' she exclaimed to the dapper man in a light blue suit.

''Quite all right,'' he replied, a friendly smile dancing his gray mustache upward. ''Walter Tilley.'' He held out a hand to her. ''Family friend and lawyer to the Delaneys. And you must be the new social director, April Cartwright.''

''Yes, I am.'' She shook his hand, then he stepped out on the porch with her.

''Matthew told me about you yesterday evening, and Mark's mentioned your name several times. It's good to have you on the team.''

She tried not to imagine what Matthew Delaney

had said about her to the lawyer. At least Walter Tilley appeared friendly enough. "Thank you, it's nice
to be part of the team."

Walter smoothed his mustache with the tip of his
index finger. "Damn shame about what happened to
Marietta."

"Marietta?"

"Marietta Lopez. She was the former social director." One of Walter's gray-speckled eyebrows raised.
"Nobody told you what happened to her?"

April shook her head. "I just assumed she quit."

"She was murdered."

April gasped, a cold wind blowing inside her.
"Murdered?"

Walter nodded. "It was the same night Mark received his injuries." April stared at him blankly, and
Walter emitted a dry chuckle. "I shouldn't be surprised that nobody has told you. The Delaneys don't
talk to many people. They barely talk to each other."

"So, what happened?"

"Nobody is certain. Apparently Mark and Marietta
met near the barn one night, and somebody hit them
both over the head with a shovel. Marietta died and
Mark sustained severe head injuries."

Severe head injuries. So that explained what had
happened to Mark and must have been the trouble
Molly had mentioned. A wave of compassion swept
through April, along with the horror of the entire situation. "Did they find out who did it?"

Walter frowned. "Sadly, no. Although the speculation is that perhaps one of the ranch hands who'd
developed a liking for Marietta committed the horrible crime." Walter shook his head. "Terrible tragedy

and followed so closely by Adam's heart attack and death.''

April's ill feelings toward Matthew were tempered by this new knowledge of the string of tragedies that had affected the family.

And Mark... What had he been like before suffering such a dreadful crime? Were the injuries he'd suffered to his brain permanent?

Walter looked at his gold watch. ''I'd better get inside. I have a meeting with Matthew, and he likes punctuality.'' He offered her another friendly smile. ''It was nice meeting you.''

''You, too.''

As April headed toward her cottage, her mind whirled with the information she'd just gained. A vicious murder, and a man left damaged. So Mark's gorgeous eyes had not always held the vagueness, his smile had not always been so wide and innocent.

A wave of heat suffused her as she tried to imagine Mark before the tragedy. The image weakened her knees.

She was already finding him far too attractive...and intriguing...in those several times when she'd seen an odd glint in his eyes that spoke of secrets, an astuteness that belied his injury.

She entered the cottage and set the thick file down on the table. ''Brian?''

''I'm in here,'' his voice wafted from his bedroom.

She entered the small room and found him unpacking the boxes that held all his earthly possessions. He'd already hung several posters on the wall using thumbtacks they'd bought that morning, and his clothes were hanging in the closet. "Looks like you've been busy while I was gone," she said.

He pulled several books from one of the boxes that were still full. "Yeah. It feels more like home with all my stuff around. You should unpack your stuff, too."

She realized he'd feel better if she unpacked and nested, so to speak. It'd give him a sense of permanency. "Maybe I'll do that this evening. Right now I have work to do. You want some lunch?"

"Nah, I'm okay. I made myself a sandwich while you were gone."

"Okay, I'll be at the table if you need anything." April left her son to his own form of nesting and settled in at the table to look over the former social director's file.

Marietta Lopez had apparently been meticulous in keeping notes of what planned activities worked and didn't work for the guests. April got out a pad and as she read, began to make notes of her own.

It was after two when Brian left his room and sat at the table across from April. "I think I'll go find Mark," he said.

"I don't think that's a good idea," April responded. Matthew's warning still rang in her ears. "Mark said he had things to do this afternoon. You can see him in the morning when you go to work at the stables."

Brian sighed and drew in a breath, but before he could voice whatever he'd intended to say, there was a knock at the door.

April answered, with Brian right at her heels. A woman and a boy about Brian's age stood at the door.

"Hi, I'm Doreen Kincheloe and this is my son, Ricky." Ricky raised a hand in greeting. "I'm the housekeeper here, and Ricky and I live in cottage one."

"Hi, I'm April Cartwright and this is Brian."

The woman smiled with friendliness. "Ricky saw Brian and insisted we come over and introduce ourselves. He was so excited to discover somebody close to his age."

"How old are you?" Brian asked Ricky.

"Almost eleven."

"I'm almost twelve," Brian replied.

"I've got a remote-control car," Ricky said. "You wanna come out and run it with me?"

Brian looked at his mother for assent. "Go on, but stay right around here," April said. Before the words were fully out of her mouth, the two boys darted away. April smiled at Doreen. "How about a cup of coffee?"

"Sure." Doreen stepped into the cottage and sat at the table while April cleared away her papers and went to make the coffee. "I can't tell you how happy we were to see you and Brian moving in. The dark months are hard on Ricky, especially now with school out and no kids his age around."

April grabbed two cups from the cupboard. "Have you worked here long?"

"Five years. But with Mr. Delaney's death I was beginning to worry that I'd have to find a new job." She swept a strand of her long, dark hair behind her shoulders. "I hear through the grapevine that you've been hired as the new social director."

"That's right, although I don't think Matthew is

particularly pleased to have me here. I was originally hired by Adam Delaney, and I seem to have gotten off on the wrong foot with Matthew.''

Doreen smiled. ''With Matthew that's not difficult to do. I think most people irritate him. So, what was your offense?''

April paused a moment to pour them each a cup of coffee, then joined Doreen at the table. ''He thinks I might try to take advantage of Mark in some way.''

''Ah.'' Doreen sipped her coffee, then shook her head ruefully. ''Mark doesn't need protection. You heard about what happened to him?''

''Just a little while ago. I met Walter Tilley, who told me what happened.''

Doreen flashed a quick smile. ''I wouldn't mind taking advantage of Mark. He's quite a hunk.'' Her teasing smile faded. ''It's sad to talk to him now, to see him having to concentrate so hard.''

''What was he like before?'' April leaned forward, vaguely surprised to discover such interest in anything she could glean about Mark.

''Of all the Delaneys, Mark was the most approachable. It was usually Mark who the help went to talk to if they had a problem, knowing he was more apt to listen than Matthew.'' Doreen paused to take another sip of the coffee. ''Mark was quick-witted and lively and genuinely nice. He's still really nice.''

''Yes, he is,'' April agreed, a flutter of warmth sweeping through her as she thought of him.

''It just takes him longer to process things now. I wouldn't ask him to help Ricky with his geometry homework, but then I can't help Ricky with geometry homework.''

April laughed, then sobered. "I understand they haven't solved the crime. Do you have any idea who is responsible?"

Doreen took another sip of her coffee. "Nobody has been arrested, although it's sort of the general consensus among the help that it was probably Lenny Boles, a ranch hand who was crazy jealous over Marietta. She was a gorgeous young woman, and she loved to flirt. She had half the cowboys around here in a dither, trying to win her affections."

"Did the sheriff investigate that possibility?" April didn't like the idea of working at a place where a murderer might be running around free.

"Yeah, but I haven't heard what has happened with the investigation. Lenny Boles wasn't working here for very long before the night of the murder, and the next day he disappeared. I think he probably saw Mark and Marietta together, flew into a jealous rage, then raced for the border and is now somewhere in Mexico."

April sat back in her chair and considered Doreen's speculation. Horrifying, senseless...and yet all too conceivable.

"Enough of this sad talk," Doreen exclaimed.

"You mentioned you've been here for five years. I assume you know the other Delaneys?" Doreen nodded. "What are they like?" April asked curiously.

Doreen raced the tip of her finger around the rim of her cup, a thoughtful frown creasing her brow. "Johnna is a lawyer in town. A defense lawyer. She's tough as nails and doesn't come to the ranch very often." Doreen's frown lifted. "Then there's Luke. If you look in the dictionary under *bad boy,* Luke's picture is there.''

April laughed. ''You're exaggerating.''

Doreen's eyes sparkled with merriment. ''Okay, maybe just a little. But Luke is every mother's nightmare and every woman's fantasy. He's a carpenter, but rumor has it his real talent is in drinking too much and bedding too many women. I notice you aren't wearing a wedding ring,'' she said, switching topics.

April nodded. ''I'm divorced. And you?'' she asked, noting Doreen's fingers were bare, as well.

A shadow momentarily stole the light from Doreen's lively dark eyes. ''My husband passed away seven months ago.''

April reached across the table and touched the woman's hand. ''I'm so sorry.''

The shadow passed and once again Doreen's eyes sparkled. ''Thanks, we're coping as best we can. Things will be easier with Brian around for Ricky to play with. And maybe sometime the four of us can plan something fun. Go to the movies or out to dinner.''

''That sounds great,'' April said warmly. A new start and a new friend. She desperately hoped the Delaneys decided to keep the ranch running.

''I'd better get out of here and let you get back to whatever you were doing.'' Doreen stood and motioned to the paperwork April had shoved aside so they could sit at the table.

The two women stepped out on the small front porch. ''You'll like working here. The Delaneys are a strange family, but they're good employers.''

Before April could ask what made them a strange

family, the sound of horse hooves filled the air. Mark rounded the corner of the workers' cottages, mounted on a huge black stallion.

Breathlessly April watched as he danced the horse in front of them. The horse reared up on its hind legs as if to dislodge the rider. But Mark appeared to be one with the horse, easily controlling the massive creature.

He tipped his hat, his eyes glittering as he held April's gaze. Then the horse came down on all fours and galloped away until man and beast were nothing more than a speck on the desert landscape.

April stared after him for a long moment after he'd completely disappeared from sight. His gaze, as it had held hers, had drawn her in, and again she'd thought she'd seen a glimmer of intelligence and more than a whisper of desire.

Was she only imagining things? Was she so pathetically lonely and in need of male companionship that she would manufacture desire in any attractive man's eyes?

"Whew. Like I said before, who cares about geometry?" Doreen exclaimed. With another friendly smile, she said goodbye and started off in the direction of her cottage.

At that moment Brian and Ricky came around the front of the building, preceded by a remote control car that buzzed and whirled in the sand.

"Hey, Mom," Brian said. "I talked to Mark a few minutes ago, and he's coming over tomorrow night for my special hamburgers."

"Brian, you should have checked with me before inviting Mark to dinner," April protested.

He looked at her as if she'd lost her mind. "Mom, we talked about it this morning in the car on the way home from the grocery store," he protested.

But that was before Matthew had warned her away from Mark, April wanted to tell her son. And that was before he'd looked at her with that hunger—a look that had caused a deep yearning on her part.

She'd only been at the Delaney Dude Ranch for two days, and already her head spun with confusion. She'd already been branded a gold digger by her boss; her son entertained a hero-worship for a man who probably didn't have the mental capacity to be a parent; and somehow that same man had managed to stir a crazy physical desire inside her.

She'd have Mark over for dinner the following night, but after that meal, when Mark had gone, she would explain to Brian that Mark wasn't a buddy and couldn't be a father figure. Mark was a worker on the ranch, brother to her boss, and the more distance she and Brian put between them and Mark, the better.

Mark tried to focus all his attention on the smooth, galloping of the horse beneath him, fighting the conflicting emotions that had driven him from the house.

The afternoon had begun innocuously enough. After arriving home from town, he'd gone to work, finding pleasure in the tasks required of him in the stables.

Around twelve-thirty he'd left the stables and headed inside the house for some lunch. It was while he was eating a sandwich that loneliness swept over him. A deep, abiding loneliness that had been with him for as long as he could remember.

He thought about going to find Matthew, whom he

knew would be in the office, working on ranch business. But as quickly as the thought entered his mind, he shoved it aside.

Matthew never talked to Mark, he talked *at* Mark. It had always been that way. Matthew did an uncanny imitation of their father, and Adam had been a cold, hard man who'd driven his sons mercilessly for the sake of the ranch.

For the sake of the ranch... The words played in his mind over and over again as he thought of his older brother. How far would Matthew go to ensure the success of the ranch? Would he dabble in something illegal?

He'd finished his sandwich with the burden of his suspicions burning in the pit of his stomach, then had decided to take a ride out to his place. It had been a while since he'd been there, and he needed to make sure no varmints, human or otherwise, had managed to breach the place.

Brian had found him in the stable and had extended the invitation for dinner the next night. Seeing the eagerness in the boy's eyes, Mark had been unable to decline.

He recognized the need in Brian as the same need he'd experienced as a boy. A need to connect with somebody, to find a place where he belonged.

Mark pushed the stallion faster, the breeze hot on his face as his mind flashed back to his childhood. Matthew had been the closest to their father. Adam had carefully groomed his eldest son in his own image.

Luke and Johnna had each other. When they were young, they'd made up their own language, shared adventures and looked upon their older brothers as their enemies.

The family dynamics had left Mark without a place—the middle son who was somehow lost to everyone else. Yes, Mark could definitely identify with the need in Brian's eyes.

A sense of peace swept through Mark as his house rose up before him. Although not huge by any standard, the three-bedroom ranch house was to have been Mark's future with Rachel.

At the time Mark had been working on it, he'd been frustrated by Rachel's lack of interest. Now he was grateful for it. She had only come here in the beginning stages of the building. But they had never made love here, had never shared moments of planning their futures here, and so the house was blessedly void of painful memories.

Mark reined in the stallion and dismounted. He tied the horse to the hitching post outside the front door, then pulled a set of keys from his pocket and went into the house.

The moment he walked through the door, he realized why he had come here—to remind himself of Rachel's loss and the inadequacies in himself that had made her look elsewhere for her future.

Like all the Delaneys, Mark realized he was not cut out for relationships, that in the end he would only hurt a woman who entered his life on a long-term basis. He shoved these thoughts aside, fighting a renewed wave of loneliness.

Mark had taken great care in deciding the floor plan of the house. The living room and kitchen were one large, open room with vast windows that looked out over the desert landscape. The furniture had been chosen to complement the aura of space and earth. A sand-colored sofa sat before the windows, cactus-green throw pillows inviting a person to sit and relax. All the furnishings were done in desert tones, colors Mark found relaxing.

He went to a wooden cabinet and pulled out a large file folder, then grabbed a can of soda from the refrigerator and sat at the wooden kitchen table.

Inside the folder were reports the sheriff had made about his investigation into Marietta's death and Mark's attempted murder. Sheriff Jeffrey Broder had left copies of the reports with Matthew, and Mark had copied them for himself.

He opened the folder and thumbed through the stack of reports. He couldn't fault Broder for not investigating thoroughly. In the days following the night of the crime, while Mark had been in the hospital, the sheriff had interviewed everyone on the ranch.

Alibis had been substantiated, potential suspects eliminated, leaving little left to go on. Mark cursed softly beneath his breath, frustration eating at him.

Was he wrong not to tell the sheriff what little Marietta had shared with him before her death? She had implied that it was possible the sheriff could be involved in whatever was going on. But what if he wasn't? Was Mark's deception making it easier for a killer to get away, easier for an illegal operation of some kind to continue?

He didn't know what to believe, didn't know who to trust, and he'd never felt so alone in his life.

He leaned back in his chair and his thoughts drifted

to April. Something about her touched him. Something about her pierced through the echo of loneliness in his heart and filled him with the promise of possibility.

Frowning, he focused once again on the report before him, trying to shove her out of his mind. But she refused to be banished. The warmth of her smile danced in his head, the beauty of her sparkling eyes was etched in his brain.

He wanted her. The force and intensity of his desire hit him like a punch in the stomach. He raked a hand through his hair and drew in a deep breath.

He knew little about her, had only spent a couple of hours with her, but he wanted her as he hadn't wanted a woman in a very long time.

Rachel's desertion had left a bad taste in his mouth. After she'd left him, he'd gone out occasionally, but hadn't any interest in the women he'd casually dated. April was different.

When he'd ridden by her cottage and she'd been standing on her porch, her cutoff shorts had displayed the sinful length of her legs—shapely legs he could easily imagine wrapped around him. Her breasts had pushed impudently against the cotton of her T-shirt, as if seeking, demanding his attention.

The words of the report before him disappeared as a vision of her face usurped them. He'd had to fight with himself in the car that morning as they'd driven to town, fight the impulse to reach out and touch the strands of her hair. He knew it would be silky soft and would hold the dizzying floral scent that surrounded her.

Still Mark knew he'd be a fool to follow through

on the desire he felt for her. First and foremost, he was playing a role that wouldn't make him particularly attractive to a woman.

Second, he had no intention of attempting to be a forever kind of man to any woman. But most important of all he had a killer to catch and a ranch to save, and those two things took precedence over anything else in his life.

Chapter 5

It was after supper when April stepped outside on her porch and stretched. She'd spent most of the afternoon sitting at the table, going over Marietta's file, and her body now protested the long period of inactivity.

The evening hours stretched empty before her. Doreen had invited Brian to go into town with them for dinner, then spend the night with Ricky. Seeing Brian's eagerness, she'd been unable to deny him the pleasure of spending time with his new friend.

She was surprised to discover that with the coming of dusk had come a cooling of the temperature. Although it was still probably in the low nineties, after a day of heat over the century mark, the nineties felt relatively cool.

Marietta's file had held a lot of interesting notes, reports and maps. It was one map in particular that held April's thoughts now. The map had depicted the structures on the ranch, with an arrow pointing to what was marked as an old barn. A note had indicated that Marietta had intended to speak to Adam about renovating the barn and using it for group activities.

April peered out across the vast landscape before her, seeking the structure in question. But there was just enough of a rise in the land to prevent her from seeing anything that might exist beyond it.

Now was a perfect time to explore a little bit, she thought. Brian was gone and there was still time before nightfall to do a little walking.

Decision made, she went back into the cottage, filled a plastic bottle with ice cubes and water and grabbed the map. Back outside again, she took off walking at a brisk pace, occasionally glancing down at the map in her hand.

She walked for about twenty minutes before slowing to a halt and taking several sips of her water. Looking ahead, she thought she spied the top of the old barn just peeking over the next hill.

Her mind whirled with possibilities for the place. The guests could be transported back and forth by a horse-drawn wagon. The activities she could offer them in a barn were endless—dances, bingo, craft classes. She suspected the biggest obstacle she'd face was getting Matthew's approval for such a project.

Still, she would face that particular chore after viewing the barn.

She picked up her pace as the barn rose before her. Although weathered to a dull gray and needing obvious cosmetic attention, the building looked sturdy and sound from the outside.

She approached the barn eagerly and saw that the large double door hung open, spilling light into what would have been a dark interior.

Stepping through the opening, she saw that the floor was completely covered in a thick layer of sand and dirt. An old broom stood in the corner as if awaiting the hand of a ranch worker.

It would be perfect, she thought with a touch of excitement. She could easily imagine a band playing in one corner while couples danced in the vast open area in the center.

No light shone through the walls, indicating to her that the building was relatively sound. She could tell Matthew that very little work would need to be done. Keeping the building as rustic as possible would only add to the charm of the activities she would plan to take place here.

The floorboards creaked beneath her feet as she walked the length of the barn, her mind whirling with all the possibilities.

A rustling noise echoed through the large building, followed by what sounded like a deep male voice emitting a single inaudible word. April froze, her heartbeat suddenly thundering in her ears.

"Hello?" she called.

Silence. Deep and profound silence.

Had she only imagined the noise? She was certain she'd heard something, and it was impossible in the cavernous building to discern where the sound had come from. Whoever had made the noise, it was obvious by the silence greeting her now that they didn't intend to show themselves.

She suddenly realized being here alone was probably not a great idea. Neither was coming here without telling somebody where she was going.

Thoughts of Marietta's murder filled her head. The killer hadn't been arrested and might possibly be hiding out right here in the old, abandoned barn.

She turned and raced for the door. It wasn't until she was outside in the waning evening light that the momentary panic faded and she felt foolish. Surely she'd just imagined the noise, or it had been an animal of some sort, scurrying to hide from her.

Unless a person was thin enough to conceal himself behind the broom handle, the barn had contained no other viable hiding place that she could immediately see.

She had panicked for nothing. Silly goose, she chided herself. She walked for what seemed like a long time, a new flutter of anxiety sweeping through her as she saw no sign of the ranch in the distance.

Night was falling quickly, painting deep shadows across the sand, transforming cacti and rocks to black silhouettes. The last place she wanted to be was lost in the desert in the hours of darkness.

She half jogged for another few minutes, the flutter of anxiety transforming to near full-blown panic when she still didn't see the ranch.

Was it possible that in her panic in leaving the barn, she'd been disoriented and taken off in the wrong direction? Had she unconsciously been veering completely off course since leaving the barn?

She'd been a fool to go exploring so far from the main buildings in the late-evening hours. Nobody would know where she had gone. With Brian staying at Ricky's house, nobody would even know she was gone until morning when Brian returned.

Icy fingers of fear danced up her spine. She stopped walking, afraid she was going in the wrong direction, afraid to worsen her stupidity by possibly moving even farther away from the ranch.

She took a sip of her water in an attempt to calm herself. Panic would serve no purpose. As she screwed the lid back on the bottle, she looked around.

In the distance she thought she saw the pale glow of a light against the encroaching night. A house?

She hurried forward, relief coursing through her. Where there was light, a house, there would be people. Surely somebody could point her in the direction of the Delaney Dude Ranch.

It was no wonder she nearly missed the presence of the house. Without the illumination spilling out the large front window, the house blended nearly perfectly into the rock cropping behind it.

As she got closer, she noticed the large horse tied to the hitching post outside the front door. A familiar horse, the one she'd seen Mark riding earlier. The horse's ears pricked up, and he snorted and pawed the ground as if the slight breeze had carried her scent to him.

With the light on in the house and the darkness of the night falling outside, April had a perfect view of Mark sitting at the kitchen table, apparently studying a pile of paperwork in front of him.

What was he doing here? Who lived here and why did Mark look so at home? She remained standing just outside the window, watching him, fascinated by the picture he presented, the picture of a man in deep concentration.

At that moment Mark looked up and through the glass, and their gazes locked. Disbelief swept over his features, and she watched as he left the table, momentarily disappeared from her sight, then reappeared at the front door.

"What in the hell are you doing out here at this time of night?" he demanded, his eyes flaming with outrage.

"I went for a walk and sort of got lost," she confessed.

"Don't you realize how unforgiving this place can be to fools?"

April stared at him in astonishment. These were not the words of a man suffering brain damage, nor were they delivered in the halting fashion she'd come to expect from him.

He frowned, his cheeks taking on a ruddy color that April perceived to be embarrassment. This only added to her confusion. "Come in." He averted his gaze from her and stepped aside to allow her to enter the house.

She stepped inside, her curiosity piqued as she entered the attractive living room. "Mark, whose house is this?" she asked.

"Mine." He moved to the round oak table and quickly slid paperwork into a folder and placed it in a kitchen drawer.

"Yours?"

When he looked at her again, he offered her the slightly vacuous smile that had been his trademark. Only this time April didn't know if she trusted it.

"This is my house, but I haven't stayed here since my accident." His words were once again halting, and he reached up and touched the back of his head as if in memory of the horrible event that had apparently changed his life.

April frowned, more confused than ever. When he'd thrown open the door and confronted her, his eyes had gleamed with sharpness and there had been no hint of simplemindedness.

He shifted from foot to foot and stuck his hands in his pockets. "Sorry I yelled at you before."

"That's all right. I should have been yelled at."

He grinned at her. "You did something stupid. Usually I'm getting yelled at for doing something stupid."

April laughed, the confusion that had rippled through her fading away. "Everyone does something stupid at one time or another." She'd done more than her share, she thought. The first stupid thing she'd done was trust the men in her life.

As always, thoughts of Derrick and her father and her utter trust in them—a trust that had been betrayed—filled her with sadness and more than a little bit of anger. As far as she was concerned, there was nothing worse than trust betrayed.

"What were you doing outside?" he asked, then added, "You want to sit?" He gestured her to the sofa.

"No thanks, I'm probably all dusty. I took a walk out this direction to look at the old barn," she explained.

"Why?"

"I thought it might be a wonderful place to hold some activities for the guests that come to the ranch."

He pulled his hands from his pockets. "It's old and dirty."

"Yes, but it could be cleaned up," she replied.

Mark shrugged. "You'd have to ask Matthew."

She nodded. "What are you doing here?"

He shrugged again. "I just like to come here sometimes." He frowned, the gesture doing nothing to detract from his attractiveness. "I come here and try to remember how I was before…"

"Mr. Tilley told me what happened to you."

"I got hurt bad, but Marietta got killed." His eyes were suddenly shadowed with the darkness of grief. "And then my daddy died." He threaded a hand through his thick, dark hair and sighed.

"Want something to drink?" he asked suddenly, and in the blink of his eyes the grief was gone.

"No, thanks. Could you point me in the right direction to get back to the ranch?"

"You can't walk back in the dark. I'm ready to leave. I'll take you back." He dug into his pocket and retrieved a set of keys.

April preceded him out of the house and watched as he carefully locked up the place, then put the keys back in his pocket. With the ease of plenty of experience, he gracefully mounted the large horse, then held out his hand to her.

"I could just walk beside you," she protested.

He grinned that slow, sexy smile that sent her pulse racing. "You afraid of horses? Or are you afraid of me?"

She felt the blush that stole over her features. "Neither," she lied. Although the truth was she was a little afraid of both.

"It's okay," he said.

Swallowing her misgivings, she reached for his hand.

In one motion that spoke of the strength of his shoulders and arms, he easily lifted her up so she straddled the saddle in front of him.

As Mark settled into the saddle behind her, she realized she had nothing to worry about where the horse was concerned. However, Mark's intimate closeness was another thing altogether.

His arms encircled her as he grabbed the reins. His masculine scent surrounded her, a heady scent that teased her senses and seemed to heat the blood flowing inside her.

She held herself stiffly erect, trying to ignore the feel of his thighs against hers, his groin pressed tightly against her bottom. The movement of the horse as they headed back to the ranch only exacerbated the intimacy of their bodies.

April was grateful he didn't try to carry on a conversation. She wasn't sure she could respond. Her entire concentration was completely used up in processing overwhelming physical sensations.

The rough rub of Mark's denim jeans against her bare legs felt erotic, the warmth of his arms surrounding her encouraged her to lean back and accept the full tactile pleasure of his body so close to hers. But she didn't. She remained rigidly upright, trying to maintain what little distance she could from him.

It wasn't until the horse began to move faster, jostling her up and down uncomfortably in the saddle that Mark pulled her back against him. "It's more comfortable if you just relax," he said, the words spoken achingly close to her ear.

Leaning flush against him might have made the ride more comfortable where the horse was concerned, but it was also too intimate, too familiar for April to fully relax.

His chest was hard and muscled against her back, and she thought she could detect his heartbeat pounding an uneven rhythm. She knew her own heart was beating faster than usual.

She was grateful when the lights of the ranch came into view, letting her know the ride would only last another minute or two. Night had completely descended, wrapping them in a blanket of darkness penetrated only by the full moon overhead.

Mark rode straight into the stable corral and drew the horse to a halt. With graceful agility, he dismounted, then reached up and grabbed her by the waist to help her down.

She came off the horse and found herself in his arms. She stepped back quickly, needing to put as much distance as possible between them. "Thanks for the ride," she said.

He nodded, his eyes glittering in the light of the moon overhead. "I'll walk you to your cottage."

"That's not necessary," she protested. Her entire body felt as if it was electrically charged. She had never been so physically attracted to a man. He affected her like no man ever had before, on a visceral level that had nothing to do with intellect. And that frightened her more than a little.

Despite her protest, he fell into step beside her as

she started toward her cottage. "Brian told me to come to dinner tomorrow," he said.

"Yes, so he said." A deep, eerie howl split the quiet of the night. "What's that?" April asked, the hairs on the nape of her neck rising.

"Coyote." Mark pointed up to the fat, almost round moon. "It's pretty close to a coyote moon."

"Coyote moon?" She looked up at him curiously as they reached her front door.

"A full moon. It makes the coyotes cry and people go crazy." He reached up and touched the back of his head. "It was a coyote moon on the night I got hurt."

"I'm sorry somebody hurt you, Mark." And she was dreadfully sorry. She could only guess at what his potential might have been, and the thought took her breath away. "Again, thank you for bringing me home," she said as she unlocked her front door.

"Don't walk in the desert again."

She turned back to him and smiled. "I promise I won't."

He nodded, then before she could even guess his intentions, he stepped toward her and kissed her. The action was so unexpected, she had no immediate defenses.

His lips captured hers with cool confidence and a mastery that, someplace in the back of her mind, astonished her. Whatever inadequacies his injury had caused him, none of them were evident in his kiss. He used his tongue to deepen the kiss, skillfully sending rivulets of fire throughout her body as his arms encircled her and pulled her tight against him.

For just a moment, a single, exquisite moment, she

responded and allowed herself to fall into the pleasure of the kiss. And just as quickly reality set in, and all the reasons she shouldn't be kissing Mark filled her head.

With a gasp she stepped back from him, her head reeling with the enormity of what they had just done. "Mark, I...you...we shouldn't have done that."

He was already walking away. "'Night, April," he said over his shoulder. "I'll see you tomorrow night."

She watched helplessly as he disappeared into the night. Her mouth still burned from the intimate contact with his. The kiss had awakened an ache deep within her, an ache she had no intention of assuaging.

She tipped her head back and stared up at the full moon. Coyote moon. The kind of moon that makes people do crazy things. It was the only explanation for her momentary lapse of judgment.

The kiss had changed things. His kiss had made her realize he was attracted to her as a man to a woman. He'd moved their tenuous relationship into an unexpected arena, and she knew it was up to her to call a halt to things before they completely progressed out of control. Tomorrow night, after Mark ate Brian's special hamburgers, she and the handsome cowboy had to have a difficult talk—for his sake and for her own, as well.

The taste of her mouth lingered while he brushed down the huge horse, as did the heat of her body pressed so close against his.

He hadn't intended to kiss her. When the impulse had struck him, he had just followed it to its pleasurable conclusion. And what a pleasure it had been. If he'd had his way he'd have carried her into her cottage and made love to her, swept all other worries and fears and bad things out of his head and simply indulged himself in the selfish pleasure of enjoying her body.

Releasing a sigh of frustration, he brushed the horse's coat with more force, trying to work out the ball of energy that burned in his stomach.

He was nearly finished with the horse when he heard voices approaching the stable. Two men stood just outside the door, apparently unaware of his presence inside.

"The boss says to prepare for a big shipment in about two weeks time." Mark instantly recognized Billy Carr's voice.

"I don't know," the second deep voice replied, a voice Mark didn't recognize. "I don't like it. Things are getting too out of hand. Nobody was supposed to get hurt."

"You can't back out now," Billy said, a mean tone in his voice. "You're in as deep as the rest of us. Don't do anything stupid."

"I'm not. All I'm saying is that we've been lucky so far. Maybe it's time to quit the whole operation."

Every muscle in Mark's body tensed, and adrenaline flooded through him. Operation? Was this what Marietta had discovered?

"We don't quit until the boss says we quit," Billy replied angrily.

Mark needed to see the man Billy was talking to. This was the first real substantial clue that something was happening here at the ranch.

He put the horse in the stall, then ambled out the door. With a grin he said, "Hi, Billy." He tensed, praying his act would serve him well.

Billy jumped in surprise and the man next to him muttered a curse beneath his breath. "Mark, buddy. I didn't know you were in there." He grabbed Mark by the shoulder and slapped him on the back. "Larry, this here is Mark Delaney."

The man named Larry muttered another curse and pulled his hat down farther as if to obscure his features. Billy laughed, an unpleasant deep chuckle and slapped Mark on the back once again. "Don't worry, Larry. There's no grain in Mark's silo, if you get my drift."

Larry frowned and eyed Mark suspiciously. Mark kept the fool smile stretched across his lips.

"So, what are you guys doing out here?" Mark asked.

"Just looking at the moon," Billy said. "It's a beauty tonight."

"Yeah, a coyote moon." Mark looked up, but shot a surreptitious glance at Larry, memorizing the man's features in his brain. He didn't know who Larry was—but he would find out before the next day was over.

"Shouldn't you get inside?" Billy asked.

"I could stay out here and watch the moon with you guys," Mark replied. Larry cursed again beneath his breath. Mark decided to take a gamble. "Are you sick, Billy?" he asked curiously.

"Never been better, why would you think I was sick?"

Mark could feel his foolish smile firmly in place. "I thought you said something about an operation."

Larry shot a worried glance to Billy. "Yeah, I've been checking into operations for you. You know, brain surgery to make you smart." He sniggered and elbowed Larry, who didn't look amused by any of it.

Mark was not amused, either. But he was definitely filled with adrenaline. "That's real nice of you, Billy."

"I'm out of here," Larry replied. "We'll talk later." He didn't wait for a reply, but instead disappeared into the shadows of the night.

"You better get inside the house, Mark," Billy said.

Mark knew there was nothing more to be learned here at the moment. "'Night, Billy."

As he walked toward the main house, his mind whirled. Marietta had been right. The brief conversation he'd overhead was his first real proof that there was something going on here, something that involved Billy and Larry—and something certainly illegal.

Drugs? They'd spoken of a shipment coming in. Was it possible the ranch was being used to run drugs between the states and Mexico?

Mark's blood ran cold at the very thought that the ranch he loved, the ranch their father had sweated blood and tears over, might be in use for nefarious purposes. Billy had talked about the boss. Who was the boss in the operation?

It would have to be somebody intimately acquainted with the ranch hands, somebody who would know who would be interested in a little illegal cash on the side. Matthew? Sheriff Broder? Any number of people could be the boss.

When Mark entered the house, he heard the voices of his sister and brothers drifting out of the family room. Their conversation wasn't the soft sounds of a family visiting, but rather strident and discordant.

Mark felt as if he were on sensory overload. First, the sweet, sensual kiss with April, then those moments of discovery with Billy and Larry. He needed time to think, time to process it all.

He started past the family room door but was halted by Matthew's voice. "Mark!"

With a sigh Mark backtracked and entered the large room. Matthew stood at the wet bar, while Luke and Johnna were seated on the sofa. "Hi," he said.

"Where in the hell have you been?" Matthew demanded, his features taut.

Mark shrugged, fighting a healthy dose of indignation. "Out," he replied.

"You know I've told you not to be out after dark," Matthew replied.

"For God's sake, Matthew," Johnna protested. "You treat Mark like he's a little boy with a curfew."

Matthew shot Johnna a warning glare, and Mark suddenly felt weary beyond belief. The undercurrents that were constantly at work between his siblings exhausted him, and it angered him that their father had never taught them how to be a real family.

"I'm tired," Mark said. He was far too tired to listen to them fight. Eventually, if they intended to hang on to the ranch, they were going to have to figure out how to get along with each other.

At the moment it didn't seem to matter that some

outside source might threaten the ranch. Mark suspected the biggest threat the ranch faced was the one from within—the Delaney siblings themselves.

Mark headed for his bedroom, the burden of his deception weighing heavy in his heart. He'd like to share the burden with somebody, but who?

The rational answer was to talk to his brothers and sister, but how could he overlook the possibility that one of them might be responsible for an illegal operation? And if Marietta had been killed to silence her, then it was possible one of the members of his own family was guilty of murder.

Chapter 6

It was easy for April, in the light of day, to rationalize away the power, the absolute wonder of Mark's kiss, as Brian chattered on about his night with Ricky and she made pancakes.

Still, that didn't keep the memory of their kiss from haunting her subconscious. Her lips had burned throughout the night, and her dreams had been erotic ones of Mark making love to her with the same mastery and skill that his kiss had possessed.

Of course the kiss had affected her, she thought as she poured the first pancake onto the awaiting griddle, it had been years since she'd been kissed at all. Like Sleeping Beauty, she'd been awakened by Mark's kiss. It had stirred emotions and sensations she'd believed forgotten.

But, of course, it was a kiss that wouldn't, couldn't be repeated. It had been an impulse on his part, and just as impulsively she had responded.

She liked Mark. She found him warm and pleasant and overwhelmingly attractive. And if she looked deep within herself, she'd have to admit that there was a part of her that was drawn to what everyone else saw as his mental inadequacies.

He appeared incapable of deception, open and uncomplicated in his thought process. So unlike Derrick, who had lied almost every time he'd spoken to her during their three-year marriage. Derrick, who had smoothly betrayed her heart.

Her heart had eventually healed, but it had taken longer to deal with the havoc he'd wreaked on her financial status. He'd used their joint credit cards to finance a lifestyle far beyond what their resources would allow. April hadn't realized how deeply they were in trouble until Derrick had left her, leaving behind a tribe of angry creditors.

And what little financial resources April had finally managed to regain, her own father had ultimately "borrowed" and lost, leaving her and Brian virtually destitute.

These two betrayals, deep and devastating, had left April with a deep wariness and a reluctance to ever trust again.

But Mark was definitely different from the men in April's past. Nonthreatening, refreshingly candid and seemingly gentle, he drew her to him.

If she were truly honest with herself, she would have to admit that he wasn't nonthreatening in a physical sense. He threatened her with the heat of his eyes, the fire of his touch, the masculine sexuality that promised pleasure beyond compare.

However, she'd been soundly warned to stay away from him.

"Mom, are you going to feed me burned pancakes?" Brian asked, pulling her from her thoughts.

She quickly flipped the smoking pancake, then added another to the griddle, trying to shove all thoughts of Mark out of her head as she finished the breakfast preparations.

"Did you take the hamburger and buns out of the freezer?" Brian asked a moment later as he stuffed a particularly large bite of food into his mouth.

"Yes, and I'll make some baked beans and deviled eggs."

"Great." Brian chewed for a moment, then continued. "I told him to be here around five."

"I'm sure he'll be here right on time," April assured her son. And after they had a pleasant meal, April had to have an unpleasant conversation with Mark.

She had to explain to him that she would be his friend, but she wouldn't kiss him anymore. She didn't want to lead him on, but she secretly realized she didn't want to lead herself on, either.

After breakfast Brian took off for the stables, and April settled down at the table with a fresh cup of coffee and Marietta's file in front of her.

It was about noon when a knock sounded at the door. She opened it to see a tall, dark-haired woman with the trademark Delaney strong features and dark gray eyes. "Hi. I'm Johnna Delaney." She gave April's hand a businesslike shake. "Matthew asked me to drop by and bring you the list of the guests who'll be arriving soon. He thought having the list might help you set up your social schedule. He also found another file of Marietta's notes.''

"Thank you,'' April took the sheath of paper from the woman.

Johnna leaned back on her heels and studied April for a long moment. "So, you're April, Mark's new friend.''

April nodded, steeling herself for yet another round of warnings from a protective sibling.

"Despite the injuries he suffered, Mark is still one of the best, kindest men in the entire state of Arizona,'' Johnna said.

April raised an eyebrow in surprise. "I agree. He's been very kind to me and my son.''

"And even though he has some problems getting his thoughts together, he's smarter than most of the cowboys working on this ranch.'' Johnna's voice held a touch of anger, an anger overlying what appeared to be a fierce protectiveness.

April offered her a tentative smile. "You're preaching to the choir, Ms. Delaney.''

Johnna offered no answering smile. "I just want to let you know that it's apparent Mark thinks a lot of you. Please don't take advantage of him, and try not to hurt him.''

April frowned irritably. "Ms. Delaney, I don't intend to take advantage of Mark in any way. He's been a friend since we've arrived. That's all, end of story.''

"It's no skin off my back if you want to be more than friends,'' Johnna countered. "But you should know one thing. This ranch is never going to make it, and when it goes under, all the Delaney money is going to go to our crazy aunt Clara who will probably spend the fortune buying little fur coats and jeweled collars for her hundreds of cats.''

April glared at the woman indignantly. ''You are the second Delaney to subtly accuse me of being a gold digger. You don't know me. You know nothing about the kind of person I am.''

April's steam grew more intense. ''And I'll tell you something else—if you and your bulldog brother, Matthew, think the only reason a woman would be attracted to Mark is for any money he might possess, you are sadly underestimating him.''

She clapped a hand over her mouth, horrified by the words that had just erupted from her. Had she really just called Matthew Delaney a bulldog?

Johnna's eyes widened as she stared at April. Then, without warning, she laughed. ''Matthew does have more than his share of bulldog tendencies, doesn't he?''

''I'm sorry, I shouldn't have said that,'' April replied, her cheeks burning with flames of mortification. Terrific, she'd probably just lost herself a job.

''No, please, don't ruin it by apologizing,'' Johnna said, her smile suddenly friendly. ''I think I'm going to like you after all, April Cartwright.'' Johnna stepped off the porch, her quicksilver smile once again gone. ''I've got to get back. Nice to have you on the team, April.''

April watched as Johnna strode away, her shoulders rigid with what appeared to be attitude.

April wasn't sure what she thought of Johnna Delaney. She appeared to be cut from the same cloth as Matthew—rather stern and with a hard gaze to her eyes. When she'd laughed, it had sounded rusty, as if laughter was an unfamiliar expression for her.

April went back to the table, carrying the sheet of paper Johnna had brought to her. Johnna had indicated that it was possible the ranch might somehow be lost. Were there financial problems? If so, then what money would go to their crazy aunt Clara? April frowned. It didn't make sense.

She poured herself another cup of coffee, deciding the Delaneys' business was not hers. She'd work here as long as possible and hopefully put enough money away so that if the ranch did go under and she lost her job, she and Brian would have a little something to fall back on.

It's no skin off my back if you want to be more than friends. Johnna's words echoed in April's mind, and once again her thoughts turned to Mark... Mark, who had kissed her with a depth and fire that had to be addressed. Despite Johnna giving her a nod of approval, April couldn't ignore Matthew's warning.

She also had to look at the bigger picture. Despite her attraction to him, Mark could never be what she needed in her life. She needed a man who could be a strong role model for Brian, a man who would be less a peer and more a father figure.

Definitely she had to tell Mark that he couldn't kiss her anymore. And she intended to address that subject this evening.

Shoving all thoughts of Delaneys out of her mind, she got back to work. It was late afternoon when Brian flew in to make his super hamburger patties. He rummaged in the spices, adding a pinch of this and a dot of that to the meat.

He hummed a nonsensical tune beneath his breath as he worked, and April feared it was the pleasure of knowing Mark was coming to dinner that had him happy.

"Mom, why don't you change your clothes before Mark gets here," Brian suggested when the hamburgers were sizzling in the skillet and the beans were bubbling in the oven.

"What's wrong with what I have on?" she asked, looking down at her worn jeans and T-shirt.

Brian frowned at her. "You just would look better in one of those dresses you have. And maybe you could fluff up your hair or something."

April raked a hair through her tousled curls and stared at her son. He's trying to matchmake, she thought in surprise. And yet, why should that surprise her?

She knew better than anyone how desperate Brian was for a father figure in his life. He had quickly grown fond of Mark. Why wouldn't he try to get the two of them together?

"Brian," she began patiently. "I know you like Mark, but there's not going to be anything between me and Mark, so you can just get that idea right out of your head."

"You don't know that," he protested as he removed the burgers from the skillet.

"I do know that," she replied firmly.

Still, a few moments later as Brian went out to wait for Mark, April went into her bedroom and changed her T-shirt, opting to wear a pale pink blouse instead.

It had nothing to do with trying to look attractive for Mark, she told herself as she finger combed her hair. She would have freshened up for anyone who was coming to dinner. She picked up a tube of lipstick, but threw it back on the dresser before she could apply any.

"Hey, Mom," Brian called from the front door. "Step outside. Mark wants to show you something."

April left her bedroom, walked through the tiny living room and stepped out on the porch. Instantly a rope whirled over her head, fell down over her shoulders and pulled tight to capture her arms against her sides.

"You got her, Mark!" Brian squealed in delight.

Mark stood some distance away, the other end of the lasso in his hands. He grinned lazily. "Sure looks like I've got her."

As Mark began to reel her in, tugging the rope to pull her off the porch and toward him, Brian clapped and cheered.

"Mark, let me go," April said, attempting to remove herself from the lasso but finding the rope too tight to work her arms out.

Ricky appeared nearby, motioning to Brian and talking excitedly about a new video game he'd just gotten. The two boys disappeared around the corner of the cottage.

Closer and closer Mark pulled April toward him, his sensual smile evoking heat through her.

"Mark, let me go," she said with a forced laugh. "I feel like a prize steer."

His grin widened. "You're much prettier than a prize steer." They were mere inches apart now, so close she could see the blue flecks that lightened the dark gray of his eyes. "I think before I let you go, I should kiss you again."

"I don't think you should do that," April replied, her breath catching in her chest.

"Why not? I like kissing you." His eyes twinkled and his smile widened. "And I think you like kissing me."

"Just because you like something doesn't mean you should do it," she protested.

"Why not?"

"Mark, please let me go."

With his eyes still sparkling evocatively, he did as she bade. As he removed the rope, his hands lightly caressed her bare arms, shooting tendrils of heat up her shoulders and down to her fingertips.

Whatever inadequacies he might suffer, they weren't apparent in his utter sexiness. She stepped back from him, back far enough that she couldn't smell his scent—the fragrance of wind and sun and a touch of spice.

"The hamburgers are ready," she said. "Brian," she yelled, and her son reappeared from around the side of cottage. "It's time to eat."

"Ricky got a new video game. After dinner can I go over and play?" Brian asked.

"We'll see," April said. Actually, that would work out perfectly. Brian could go to Ricky's house while April had her difficult talk with Mark.

She had to make him understand that they could be friends. But friends didn't kiss with such depth and longing, and friends didn't look at each other as if they wanted to devour the other.

As the heat of his touch slowly ebbed, she reiter-

ated in her mind that, definitely, it was time to have
a talk with Mark.

As Mark sat at the table with mother and son, he
studied April. She looked particularly fetching in a
feminine pink blouse that brought a blush of color to
her cheeks.

A surge of desire welled up inside him, and his
fingers tingled with the tactile memory of the feel of
her skin as he'd removed the lasso from around her.

"So...what do you think?" Brian asked, interrupting Mark's thoughts. He pointed to the hamburger
Mark was eating.

"It's really good, Brian." Mark smiled at the boy,
who eyed him eagerly. "You're a real good cook."

Brian beamed beneath the praise. "I couldn't make
them like I usually do 'cause we didn't have all the
spices I needed, but I did the best I could."

"They're terrific, Brian," April said, her gaze soft
and loving as it rested on her son.

A flash of memory swept through Mark...a memory of his own mother gazing at him in that very same
way. The memory surprised him with its vividness.

He'd been five years old when his mother had died
giving birth to Johnna and he hadn't realized the
depth of his deprivation until this moment, seeing
April gaze at Brian.

He wondered how different his relationship with
his siblings and his father would have been had his
mother lived. Would she have provided the warmth,
the commitment to family, the unconditional love that
had been lacking under his father's care?

He shoved these thoughts aside, knowing nothing

could be gained by wondering what if. What seemed more important at the moment was trying to decide if he could trust April Cartwright with his secret.

"I met your sister today," April said.

Mark raised an eyebrow. "You did?"

She nodded. "She brought by a detailed list of the first guests who'll be here. She seemed very nice."

Mark almost laughed aloud. Few people found Johnna nice. She was usually abrasive, hardheaded and driven. If she had been nice to April, then there was probably an ulterior motive.

"Johnna's a lawyer," Mark said. "A defense lawyer, but now she has to spend part of her time working the ranch because that's what my father's will says."

"Were you sad when your dad died?" Brian asked.

Mark hesitated before replying. It would be easy to say no, to tell the boy that Adam had been a heartless bastard and the world was better off without him.

That was what Mark wanted to believe, because it made his father's death easier to accept. It made the poor connection between them his father's fault and not Mark's.

"Yeah, I was sad," he finally answered, and in his simple statement, he recognized the truth. He was sad, sad for all the lost years, sad for what he and Adam would never have.

"My dad isn't dead, but he makes me sad," Brian said softly.

Mark saw the pain that darkened April's lovely eyes at her son's words. He wondered what had happened to her marriage.

For some reason the sadness in her eyes and the

gentle touch of her hand to her son's touched him deeply. Through the rest of the meal the talk remained pleasant. Both Brian and April asked him questions about the daily running of the ranch when guests were present, and he answered them as well as he could if he were truly suffering some sort of brain damage.

It was frustrating as hell to pretend he didn't have the mental faculties of an intelligent man. He found himself watching every word, carefully weighing each response.

He wished he could just throw caution to the wind, explain the whole subterfuge to April. But he knew better than anyone that the safest course of action would be for him to maintain silence. Still, the burden of his secret weighed heavily on him.

For the past three weeks, since making the decision to appear addled, Mark had been forced to live an existence of isolation. In those weeks he hadn't had a truly meaningful discussion with anyone, nor had he been able to relax for a moment, fearful that he might somehow give himself away.

They were clearing the table when a knock sounded at the door. Brian answered and instantly turned to his mom. "It's Ricky. Can I go over to his house and play his new video game with him?"

April nodded, then looked at her watch. "Okay, but be home by eight-thirty."

Almost before the words were out of her mouth, Brian shot out the door. "Thanks, Mom. See you in the morning, Mark," he said over his shoulder, then he pulled the door closed, leaving Mark and April alone in the small cottage.

April flashed him what appeared to be a slightly

nervous smile as she put the last dish away in the cabinet. "Sit down, Mark. We need to have a talk." She gestured to the sofa.

"A talk?" He eyed her curiously as he sat.

She joined him on the sofa, her expression somber. Mark's curiosity was piqued. He couldn't imagine what she needed to discuss with him.

She raked a hand through her short, pale curls and drew a deep breath. "Mark, you mustn't kiss me anymore." Her cheeks instantly flamed with color.

"Why not? I liked kissing you, and you liked kissing me."

Her blush intensified. "That's not the point." She sighed and once again threaded a hand through her curls. "You're a Delaney, and that means you're one of my bosses. It isn't good to have a relationship with a boss."

"I'm not a boss," Mark scoffed. "Matthew is the boss. I just work with the horses."

"Mark, you're a very nice man, but it isn't appropriate for you to kiss me anymore." She averted her gaze from his.

He wanted to kiss her again now, at this very moment, with the blush on her cheeks and her discomfort with the conversation so obvious.

He wanted to kiss her and watch the green of her eyes deepen and taste the sweetness of her lips. His fingers itched with the need to caress her soft skin, to feel the sensual softness of her blond curls.

"Matthew doesn't want us kissing," she finally said, and looked at him once again.

He raised an eyebrow in surprise. "He told you that?"

"Not exactly," she hedged. "But he said he didn't want me taking advantage of you."

"Taking advantage…" Mark cursed inwardly. For years Matthew had virtually ignored Mark. But now, after a knock on Mark's head, Matthew was suddenly the poster boy for big brothers of the world. "Matthew is not my keeper, and he has no right to involve himself in my personal life." Instantly he recognized he'd been too eloquent in his statement.

April's eyes narrowed slightly, and he saw a trace of suspicion in the depths. "He's your brother and he worries about you," she finally said.

"Matthew doesn't worry about anything but the ranch," he countered, his tone sharper than intended.

April frowned. "You mentioned something earlier about your father's will forcing your sister to spend time on the ranch."

Mark nodded and saw her relax as the conversation moved away from the reasons he shouldn't kiss her. "In his will, it's stipulated that all of us have to spend twenty-five hours a week working the ranch for a year or else the ranch is sold and everything goes to our aunt Clara." Again he realized he wasn't using the words of a man who found thinking and speaking difficult. But April didn't seem to notice.

"And that's why Matthew wasn't sure if the ranch would remain open or not?" she asked.

"Yeah. We'll never make it the whole year," Mark said, voicing what he'd subconsciously known since the moment the will had been read.

"Why not?"

Mark sighed. "Johnna hates the ranch and everything to do with it. She and Matthew butt heads about nearly everything.'' Mark suddenly realized why Johnna had been nice to April. If Matthew had indicated he didn't like April, or didn't trust her, then Johnna would take April under her wing just to be perverse.

''What about your brother Luke?'' April asked curiously.

''Luke doesn't care much about anything but his guitar and having a good time. He and Johnna will never make it the whole year. The Delaney Dude Ranch will eventually be sold.''

''And what will you do if that happens?'' Her voice was soft with empathy.

He was surprised by her question. He'd expected her to worry about what she would do if that happened. ''I don't know,'' he replied, and stared thoughtfully at the wall.

His father had always told him he wasn't good for anything other than dealing with the horses, and without the ranch there would be no horses for him to tend. ''I try not to think about it.''

April placed her hand on his forearm, her gaze impossibly soft as it searched his face. ''I'm sure you'll be just fine no matter what happens.''

He covered her hand with his and smiled at her. ''I sure have a strong need to kiss you again.''

She withdrew her hand as if his skin were on fire, and again a deep blush engulfed her features. She stood and stepped away from the sofa, but not before he saw a flare of desire spark in her eyes. ''Mark, we just went through all of that,'' she exclaimed.

Mark stood and approached her, standing so close to her he could feel her heat, see the emerald flecks that made her eyes so impossibly green. "You said Matthew didn't want you taking advantage of me. But you didn't say anything about me taking advantage of you."

Before she could protest, before she could reply in any fashion, he took her into his arms and covered her mouth with his.

For a brief moment she remained stiff, but as his tongue deepened the kiss, she softened, sweetly yielding to his embrace and the heat their mouths produced.

Mark pulled her more tightly against him, loving the way her soft curves felt against the hard planes of his body. His hands smoothed up her back, beneath her blouse, touching her impossibly smooth skin.

At that instant he knew kissing her wouldn't be enough. He wouldn't be satisfied until he touched every inch of her sweet skin, felt her nakedness next to his, possessed her completely.

"April," he whispered against her throat as his lips left hers. "Sweet April." She gasped with pleasure as his mouth blazed a trail down the side of her neck.

He wanted her so badly, he ached inside. He wanted to whisk her into his arms, take her into her bedroom and love her until they both were lost in a haze of passion.

"April, my brain damage. It isn't real. I've been faking it." He hadn't meant to blurt it out so starkly, but he suddenly realized there was no way he could take his caresses any further, no way he could make love to her without telling her the truth.

Instantly April stiffened against him, then stepped away. He held his breath as he saw first disbelief, then anger, darken April's eyes.

Chapter 7

April stared at the handsome cowboy standing before her, trying to make sense of what he'd just said. But it was difficult to think with the imprint of his mouth still burning hers, with the memory of his warm hands on the bare skin of her back. "What are you talking about?" she asked.

He sank back on the sofa and patted the space next to him. "Please, come sit down and let me explain."

Grudgingly she did as he asked, perching on the very edge of the sofa and staring at him in bewilderment. "What do you mean, you've been faking it?"

"I mean just what I said. I don't have any lingering brain damage. I was not turned into a simpleton by the shovel that hit me."

April searched his face, her mind working to make sense of what he'd just said. Shock ricocheted through her, yet on some level deep inside her, she wasn't so surprised after all.

She thought of those odd moments when she'd thought she'd seen intelligence radiating from his eyes. One minute his gaze would be vague, like soft, fuzzy dove wings, and the next it would be gunmetal-gray and sharp as twin bullets. His conversations with her had been confusing, as well. Sometimes she'd forget that he had brain damage.

"Then why...why are you pretending otherwise?" she asked incredulously. As her shock dissipated, a surge of anger welled up inside her.

"Because it's the only way I know to catch the person who killed Marietta and tried to kill me." He raked a hand through his hair. "Marietta was the social director before you. I met her one night out by the barn and—"

April interrupted him with a wave of her hand. "Walter Tilley told me all about it." She frowned, trying to focus on his words instead of the deep sense of betrayal that swept through her. After all, Mark Delaney was nothing to her. Why should she be angry that he'd lied to her when he'd lied to his own family, as well?

The answer came swiftly. Because he had just kissed her until her senses spun, because he had stirred in her a deep want that would have made it easy for her to give in—and it had all been done from a point of deception.

"What about your family? How could you keep up the pretense with them?" She couldn't imagine any reason strong enough to justify what he'd done, what he apparently intended to keep doing to his brothers and sister.

He frowned and his eyes darkened to the deepest

shadows of night. "Because I don't know if I can trust them."

Again April was struck by how odd the relationship of the Delaney siblings was. Odd and somehow sad. Of course, she'd trusted her own father, and that had been an enormous mistake. "I thought the sheriff knew who had hurt you," she said. "Some worker who disappeared after that night."

"Lenny Boles," Mark replied. "That's who the sheriff thinks did it."

"But you don't think so?"

"No, I don't. I don't know what happened to Lenny, but I don't think he had anything to do with Marietta's death and my injuries." He frowned and rubbed his forehead, as if suffering a headache. "Lenny was a loner and something of a gutless worm. Branding cattle made him ill. I can't imagine him having the stomach for bashing somebody over the head."

"Then who?" April couldn't help asking. It was much easier to focus on the crime that had occurred than her warring emotions concerning his confession.

"I don't know. That's what the addle-minded pretense is all about." He leaned toward her, his gaze more intense than she'd ever seen it before. That intensity nearly stole her breath away.

She'd thought him handsome before, with the characteristic vagueness in his eyes, but with the sharpness of intelligence radiating from their depths, he was devastating.

"Something is going on here at the ranch...something I can't get a handle on. But Marietta knew about it, and the night she tried to tell me what was going on, she was killed and I almost was killed, as well.''

April drew in a deep breath and averted her gaze, finding it difficult to concentrate on what he was saying while looking at him. She was still too close to the intimacy they had shared only moments before. ''And you don't have any idea what might be going on?''

''Possibly drug running or selling.'' He told her about the conversation he'd overheard in the stables. ''Whatever it is, I know Billy Carr is involved and a man named Larry that he was talking to. What I need to find out is exactly what is taking place here and who the boss is.''

''But why the need to pretend that you have brain damage?'' April asked, trying to understand.

''Because all the ranch hands talk freely in front of me now. They think I'm too stupid to understand what they're saying. I've already learned that Jacob Sinclair regularly steals grain and Timothy Franklin skims off the top whenever he goes to town for supplies.''

''But stealing grain and skimming a little cash isn't the same as murder and attempted murder,'' she protested. ''Isn't this something you should take to the sheriff? Let him handle whatever might be going on?''

''No.'' The succinct reply was followed by a deep sigh that for some reason resonated inside April. ''This is something I have to do myself.'' For the first time April saw something dark, almost haunting in his gaze. ''The last thing Marietta said to me before she was killed was to trust nobody—not my family and not the sheriff. She was adamant about it. I...I don't know who to trust.''

April's anger resurfaced inside her. She stood and walked several paces away from the sofa, then turned to face him once again. ''Why are you telling me all this? Why did you feel the need to confess this secret to me?''

He grinned, the darkness she'd momentarily seen gone beneath the charm of his smile. ''Because I figured if I was going to kiss you anymore, then we shouldn't have any secrets between us.''

''I'm being serious,'' she replied curtly, angered further by his flippant reply.

He leaned forward and raked a hand through his thick, dark hair. His smile was gone as he studied her. ''Because for some reason I knew I could trust you,'' he said softly. ''Because I haven't had a deep, meaningful conversation with anyone since I started this charade.'' He shrugged. ''Because I just wanted— needed you to know that I was okay.''

April became aware of a headache throbbing at her temples. ''Okay, great. You've shared your secret with me. Now I think it's time for you to leave.''

His eyebrows quirked up with surprise. ''You're angry.''

''Don't be ridiculous,'' she replied. ''I don't know you well enough to be angry with you.'' She sighed, her headache intensifying. ''Mark, I'm sorry that somebody hurt you, but I'm not sure I agree with what you're doing, fooling everyone. Still, it's really none of my business.''

She opened the door, allowing in a wave of warm, evening air. ''I don't want to know about murder and deception. I'm a single mother just wanting to make a decent life for me and my son. Now, I think it best if we just say good-night.''

He stood and walked toward her, his expression unreadable. He stopped when he was close enough that she could smell his evocative scent, close enough that she could feel his body heat. ''April...I'm sorry if I made a mistake in confiding in you. It wasn't my intention to add to whatever burdens you're carrying.''

His apology effectively banished the anger that had momentarily gripped her. ''You don't have to worry about me telling anyone. Your secret is safe with me.''

He smiled—that damnable smile that shot heat through her veins. ''I wasn't worried. I told you a minute ago I knew I could trust you.'' He stepped outside, then turned back to her. ''Tell Brian his hamburgers were terrific and I'll see him tomorrow.''

She nodded, grateful when he turned and left. She immediately closed the door and went to the kitchen cabinet for some aspirin. She got a glass of water, swallowed two tablets, then sat at the table, her mind whirling with everything she had just learned.

No brain damage. The whole thing was nothing but a sham. Incredible. And yet, as she thought back over the times she'd spent with Mark, the clues had been there.

She rubbed her temples, wondering again about the Delaney family dynamics. Why would Mark choose to tell a virtual stranger his secret instead of sharing it with his family? Why would he take the suspicions of Marietta, a ranch worker, over his family?

She thought of that first kiss they had shared, a kiss that had thrilled her down to her toes. It had been the kiss of a man skilled at physical pleasure. Yet at the time she had felt slightly guilty, worrying that somehow she might take advantage of Mark and his condition.

A touch of anger reappeared. He'd taken advantage of her. He'd kissed her the first time and this evening under false pretenses, pretending to be something that he wasn't. She'd been drawn to him because she'd thought he was different—more innocent and pure. She now realized those attributes had been sleight of hand, tricks of the light. Lies.

She suddenly recognized that her anger wasn't really anger at all. Rather what she felt was disappointment. She was disappointed to realize that Mark was just another male who was exceptionally good at deception.

By the next morning her headache was blessedly gone, and she resolutely shoved all thoughts of Mark Delaney out of her mind.

She spent the morning at the table with the list of guests who would soon be arriving, working up the schedule of activities she needed to have approved by Matthew.

As she opened Marietta's thick file, she remembered what Mark had told her the night before—that Marietta had known something was going on at the ranch and she'd met with Mark to tell him what she knew.

Was it possible Marietta had written something down in the file April now possessed? There was an impossible amount of paperwork in the two manila folders. April hadn't even begun to get through it all.

She stared at the file. Should she mention them to Mark? Maybe something in the files could help him solve the mystery.

She hesitated. Did she really want to get involved with any of this? After all, it certainly wasn't her place to help Mark figure out what was going on at the ranch. And yet, if it were something illegal, some activity that put them all at risk, wasn't it her civic responsibility to do what she could?

She shook her head ruefully at this thought. Civic responsibility, indeed. The truth of the matter was she couldn't get Mark out of her head, couldn't forget the deep torment she'd seen in his eyes. She wanted to help him. It was as simple—and as complicated—as that.

Making up her mind, she left the cottage and went in search of him.

She found Brian outside the stables, raking a portion of a corral with a wide rake. "Where's Mark?" she asked her son. He stopped his work for a moment and pointed toward the stable.

Entering the building, she was greeted with the sounds and smells of horses. Hooves pawed the ground, nostrils snorted the air, and soft whinnies greeted her as she passed each of the stalls.

She heard Mark before she saw him. His deep voice was soft and caressing. "It's all right, sweet girl. I'm not going to hurt you."

Stepping toward a large work area, she spied him brushing a horse's mane. The horse was obviously nervous, sidestepping the touch of the comb.

April didn't speak for a moment, but instead simply watched. Today, instead of being clad in his usual blue jeans, he wore a pair of black denim jeans that made his legs look longer, leaner. Beneath his gray T-shirt, his bicep muscles bulged and danced as he worked to both maintain control of the horse and accomplish the combing.

"Mark," she called softly, irritated that the very sight of him swept a whisper of heat through her.

He looked up from the horse, his lips curving with pleasure. "April. Are you looking for Brian? He's outside."

"No," she replied. "I wanted to talk to you."

"Just a minute. Let me put Muffin here away." He led the horse to a nearby stall, his soothing, soft talk continuing as he settled the horse in the small enclosure.

April wondered if he would use that same soft, caressing voice when making love. Would he caress his lady with the same tenderness that he used on the animals?

As he approached where she stood, she shoved her disturbing thoughts away. She didn't intend to find out if Mark Delaney was a tender lover.

"So, what's up?" he asked, his gaze warm as it lingered on her face. "Have you decided to forgive me?"

"I told you last night that there's nothing to forgive. I wanted to talk to you because while I was doing a little work this morning, I had a sudden thought about Marietta."

Mark glanced around, then took her by the arm and

pulled her toward a door. April realized he didn't want anyone to hear their conversation.

He opened the door and pulled her inside a tiny closet. Reaching above his head, he tugged on a chain that lit the dim lightbulb overhead.

April was instantly aware of their proximity, forced by the small enclosure. Her breasts were mere inches from his broad chest, and if she tilted her head slightly back, his lips would be within easy reach.

"Now, what did you want to tell me?" His voice was a low whisper, his breath smelling of mint as it fanned her face.

"I've been looking through Marietta's file that Matthew gave me, and it's obvious that she was an extensive note maker." She stared at his chest as she spoke, not wanting to look up into his eyes. "The file is huge, and I've only managed to get through about an eighth of it. I was thinking maybe if Marietta had suspicions about something going on here at the ranch, she might have written something down in the file."

"I've been through most of her file," he replied.

"But your sister brought me another file. Have you seen it?"

He shook his head. "No, I haven't, but I'd like to." With his forefinger beneath her chin, he tilted her head so their gazes met. "I know this is asking a lot, but could I come to your place and go through the second file? Maybe you could help me figure things out. Will you help me?"

She wanted to tell him no, wanted to tell him she didn't want to get more deeply involved with him.

But seeing the sweet heat in his eyes, she was powerless to deny him.

Besides, he was only asking her to go over some papers with him. What harm could come from that?

"All right," she agreed reluctantly, eager to get away from his overwhelming nearness. "Come to my place tonight after dinner, and we can go through all of it."

"Great. About seven?"

She nodded and reached to open the door. He stopped her by placing his hand over hers on the knob. "April, I really appreciate it."

For a moment she thought he was going to kiss her. His eyes darkened and she saw the intended kiss on his features as his face moved closer to hers.

Her breath caught in her chest as she realized how badly she wanted him to kiss her again. And as that realization made itself known, she quickly turned the doorknob and stepped out of the closet.

"I'll see you tonight," he said.

She nodded and left the stables. As she walked back toward her cottage, she wondered what it was about Mark Delaney that sent her senses reeling, that made her think of hot nights and stolen kisses, of sweaty bodies and whispered sighs.

She would help him go through Marietta's file, but that was where their interaction halted. The last thing she needed in her life was a man who'd already proven he was adept at deception.

It was exactly seven when Mark walked from the main house toward April's cottage. He was looking forward to spending the evening with her, especially since she now knew the truth about him.

When he'd initially told her he was faking his injuries, he'd been surprised by her anger. Although she'd claimed that she didn't know him well enough to be angry, that it was none of her business and therefore she couldn't be angry, her outrage had been obvious.

He'd thought about that outrage all evening after leaving her, and it had finally dawned on him that kissing her while pretending to be mentally challenged had been not only unfair, but wrong.

Had she responded to his kiss simply from compassion?

From pity? Had she been afraid of offending "poor Mark" by rebuffing his kiss?

He frowned. Surely it hadn't been compassion he'd tasted on her lips. It had been the heat of desire, the sweetness of a response that had nothing to do with pity.

As he neared her place, his heart seemed to skip a beat in anticipation. He was nearly as eager to talk to her as he was to kiss her again.

It had been impossible to talk to her, really talk to her while functioning beneath the weight of his pretense. It would feel good to be able to be himself for a little while.

April answered his knock with a tentative smile and gestured him in. The cottage retained the scents from their dinner, tangy tomato sauce with a hint of garlic.

She was dressed in jeans and a short-sleeved peach-colored floral blouse that emphasized her full breasts.

"I made a pot of coffee," she said, and gestured

to the table, where a thick manila envelope sat in the center. "The paperwork is all there, so we can get started right away."

She obviously intended the evening to be strictly business. "Where's Brian?" he asked as he sat at one of the chairs at the table.

"Outside with Ricky. Those two have become best of friends. Cream or sugar?" she asked as she poured coffee into two awaiting cups.

"No, just black."

She joined him at the table, sitting across from him rather than next to him. Even with the relative distance between them, he caught the scent of her fragrance, a sweet floral scent that evoked thoughts of spring and budding life.

"I've gone through the first thirty pages or so," she said as she opened the folder. "I've found grocery lists, notes about errands run…the whole file seems to be a mix of business and personal notes."

He noticed her hands, pretty hands with slender fingers and blunt-cut nails covered in a pearly pink polish. If he'd still been pretending to be ill, he would have blurted out how pretty they were. Now he kept the thought to himself, realizing that there had been a certain freedom in his chosen role.

"We'll probably find nothing here that can help you, but I thought it might be worth looking at." She finally gazed at him.

"It was a good thought." He smiled. "Let's get started."

They worked for almost two hours straight, interrupted only when Brian and Ricky came to check in, then disappeared into Brian's bedroom.

The whole time Mark was trying to focus on the notes before him, his head was filled with April's nearness. Her scent stirred him to distraction. The sight of her hands shifting through papers made him wonder what those delicate fingers would feel like dancing over his skin.

It was close to nine when Mark decided he'd had enough for one night. The words had begun to dance dizzily as his eyes grew tired of the meticulous work.

"Why don't we take a break," he said, and shoved back from the table.

"Sounds good to me. You want more coffee?"

"No, thanks, I'm fine." He stood and stretched his arms overhead, then gestured toward the front door. "Want to step outside and get a little air?"

"Sure, just let me tell the boys where we're going." She walked over to Brian's door and knocked. "Mark and I are going to step outside for a few minutes," she told her son when he answered. "Why don't you and Ricky go ahead and get into your pajamas."

A moment later April and Mark stepped outside into the night. He sat on the porch stoop, and she joined him there, smiling self-consciously as their shoulders momentarily bumped against each other.

She drew a deep breath. "I still can't get over how warm it stays at night after the sun goes down," she said softly.

"After you've been here awhile you begin to appreciate the subtle nuances of temperature." He looked at her curiously. "What brought you here? You mentioned that your father knew my father. Had he been here as a guest or did you visit as a child?"

"Neither." She lifted her face to peer at the sky, and the moonlight washed over her features, giving them a luminous glow. "After my father's death, I was going through his paperwork and found a letter and a brochure from your father. The letter indicated that the two men had been friends for years, and Brian and I desperately needed a new start, so I called your father, who offered me the position as social director."

"You said you needed a new start. Did something happen?" He wanted to know all about her, where she'd been in the past, where she wanted to go in the future.

She pulled her gaze from the moon and instead focused on the dark landscape before them. "Brian and I were living with my father, and we discovered after his death that the house was heavily mortgaged and he had day-traded away everything, including all of my savings."

In the last five words she spoke, he heard a wealth of pain and deep betrayal. That was what family had the power to do, he thought. To hurt. And that was why he would never have a family of his own, never bind himself to anyone. He didn't ever want the responsibility of hurting somebody as only a loved one could do.

He was a Delaney, and Delaneys didn't "do" relationships…at least not long-term ones.

"Sounds like a tough break," he said sympathetically.

"It was devastating," she admitted. She sighed, a sigh that reflected a despair of the soul, a sigh that somehow touched a chord of response in him.

But that was ridiculous, he scoffed inwardly. There was no despair inside him. He was angry about the crime that had taken place here at the ranch, worried about the repercussions of what Marietta had known. He was tormented by the knowledge that there was a possibility one of his family members was involved. There were even times he would admit he suffered a touch of loneliness. But there was certainly no soul ache inside him.

She straightened her shoulders, as if in doing so she'd gather inner strength, and smiled at him. "It was devastating, but I'm a survivor. I've been through bad times before, and I'll get through this time, as well."

Her smile was bewitching: her full lips curved upward and her eyes sparkled with determination. The gesture lasted only a moment, then faded. "It's Brian I worry about. He's had so little stability in his life so far."

"He seems like a good kid. Sometimes a difficult childhood makes a strong man."

"I suppose," she agreed thoughtfully. "But that doesn't mean a loving mother would consciously create a difficult childhood for her child."

"I wouldn't know about that," he replied. "My mother died giving birth to Johnna. I was five when my mom died." Again a nebulous memory whispered across his consciousness—the memory of his mother's laughter, warm and musical.

April's hand on his arm banished the echo of memory. "That must have been terrible for you...all of you, growing up without a mother. And how terrible for your father to carry the burden of four children alone.''

"Yeah, well, he didn't exactly qualify for father of the year," Mark said unevenly. He drew a deep breath to still the emotions that suddenly simmered close to the surface, alien emotions that were disturbing and unsettling.

"What are you going to do if we don't find anything in Marietta's notes?" she asked.

He stretched his legs out in front of him, grateful for the switch of topic. He didn't want to think about fathers and families. "Keep doing what I'm doing and hope I stumble onto something. I spent the afternoon in town, trying to find out about the Larry that Billy Carr was talking to in the stables the other night."

"And what did you find out?"

"That his name is Larry Greco. He's been in town about six months and has no visible means of support. He has a reputation as a loner with a hot temper."

"You learned all that this afternoon?" she asked, searching his features in amazement.

He grinned. "I told you, when people think you're not all there, they tend to run off at the mouth in front of you."

Suddenly he didn't want to discuss Billy Carr or Larry Greco. He didn't want to think about the ranch or their respective pasts. He'd much rather talk about how her hair shone as if gilded by the moonlight. He'd rather focus on how her lips, slightly shiny in the lunar light, seemed to beckon him closer, tease him with possibilities.

"Tell me something, April Cartwright," he began. He leaned closer to her, so that he could once again smell the floral scent of her, feel it wrapping his senses in sweet petals. "Have you ever been kissed by a cowboy no longer pretending to be brain damaged beneath an Arizona coyote moon?"

Her eyes flared bright, then she smiled, a teasing, smile that lit a fire in the pit of his stomach. She tilted her head to one side as if thinking. "No," she finally replied. "And I've never walked buck-naked down Main Street, either."

Before he could guess her intent, she jumped up and opened the door. "Good night, Mark." Without waiting for his reply, she disappeared into the cottage, leaving him sitting alone beneath the full coyote moon.

Chapter 8

Sheriff Jeffrey Broder eyed Mark from across the expanse of Matthew's study. Matthew stood to the left of the sheriff, looking as imposing and tense as Mark had ever seen.

"I just stopped by to do a little follow-up, Mark," Sheriff Broder explained. "I was hoping that with a little time and a little healing, maybe you would remember something else about the night you got hurt."

"I thought you were certain that Boles was guilty," Matthew interjected. "Have you found him?"

"Not yet. We put out an APB on him. If he shows his face around these parts or anywhere else in the country, he'll be stopped and detained for questioning."

"If you're certain he's your man, then why are you bothering Mark again?"

Mark studied Matthew with eyes of suspicion. Matthew had seemed more on edge, more irritable lately than Mark had ever seen him. Was it because he was "the boss" of whatever illegal operation was functioning here at the ranch? Was it possible he was feeling the heat of this investigation and getting nervous?

"A case is never closed until somebody is serving time," the sheriff replied. "I'd be remiss in my duties if I didn't talk to Mark again." Broder looked from Matthew to Mark. "Anything new to add?"

Was it possible the sheriff wanted to know what Mark remembered in order to assess if Mark was a threat? Mark had never felt so torn in his life. He was growing weary of his game, a game that had yielded far too few clues.

But he was aware that trusting the wrong person might not just be a mistake but could cost him his life. He shrugged and smiled helplessly at Sheriff Broder. "I don't remember anything," he said.

All he needed was a little more time, he told himself. Billy and Larry had mentioned a shipment coming in, in two weeks time. That meant sometime in the next ten to twelve days something would be happening somewhere on the ranch. And Mark intended to patrol the ranch as best he could to see what he could discover.

"Are you sure there's nothing, Mark?" Sheriff Broder asked. "Anything…any little thing might help."

"He's answered your questions, Jeffrey. I don't want him upset." Matthew's voice held a steel edge.

Again suspicion swept through Mark. Dear God,

Matthew, he thought desperately. Have you done something terrible in order to keep the ranch? Have you sold your soul to keep Father's dream alive?

He wished he knew his brother well enough to discount his suspicions, but he didn't.

At the moment there was only one person in the world he trusted—April.

The next three days flew by as April and Brian settled into a comfortable routine. In the daytime Brian worked with Mark in the stables and April planned her activities for guests. After her schedule had been approved by Matthew, she was given a budget and spent much of her time on the phone, ordering a variety of equipment and special foods.

Most evenings Brian and Ricky played together and Mark and April sat at the table and plowed through Marietta's files. After reading page after page of notes, they would break for the night and sit outside and talk.

It was nearly seven and April stood at the window, watching for Mark's familiar figure to approach the cottage. It bothered her that she'd come to look forward to his evening visits, that she was discovering he was just as Doreen had described to her—quick-witted, lively and genuinely nice.

She frowned as a car pulled up out front. The back door opened and Brian flew out and into the cottage. "Mom, Ricky's mom wants to know if I can go to town with them, then spend the night at Ricky's house. Please, Mom. Please let me."

April smiled, her heart full as she saw the happiness that lit Brian's features. There was nothing like a best friend to make a boy's life right. It warmed April's heart to know Brian had found a best friend.

"Let me check it with Doreen," she replied. Together mother and son left the cottage. April greeted Doreen with a friendly smile. "I hear you've got big plans for the night."

Doreen laughed. "Yeah, running errands and doing laundry. I told the boys if they were good while I'm doing all that, we'd maybe go bowling or go to a movie, then Brian could stay the night."

"Please, Mom," Brian appealed.

"Are you sure you want to do this?" April asked Doreen.

Doreen shrugged. "Sure. Actually, two are easier than one. You're really doing me a favor if you let Brian come with us. It will be late when we get back from town, so he might as well just bunk at our house for the night."

April looked at her son. "What are you waiting for?" She laughed as he scrambled into the back seat with Ricky. The two boys punched each other in their arms, a ritual male-bonding thing April had never understood.

She waved as Doreen pulled away, then turned to see Mark approaching. As always her heart jumped at the sight of him. She'd never seen a man wear a pair of jeans better, had never noticed on another man how the tilt of a hat could suggest such blatant sensuality.

"Where are they off to?" he asked, gesturing to the car that was nothing more than a ball of dust in the distance.

"Town," she replied, then smiled. "Brian and Ricky have practically become joined at the hip."

Mark's face beneath the hat was shadowed from the evening cast of the sun. He frowned, the gesture appearing to deepen the shadows on his features. "It's good to see the two of them together. Boys need friends. My father never allowed us to have any."

They'd begun walking toward her porch, but at his words she stopped and turned to look at him once again. "Your father never allowed you to have friends? Why not?"

He shrugged. "Who knows? Maybe he was afraid we'd find out other fathers were different from him. Maybe he was afraid somehow having friends would undermine his total authority over us. Who knows what forces drove my father to be a mean, miserable man?"

He'd intimated before that Adam Delaney had been a difficult father, but he'd never come right out and said it until this moment.

April knew all about relationships with difficult fathers, although she had finally come to terms with her relationship with her own.

"Not everyone gets a lucky draw when it comes to fathers," she said as they stepped up on the porch.

He opened the door, the dark shadows still clinging to his features beneath the glare of the kitchen light even after he removed his hat. "We should get through the last of that file this evening," he said, changing the subject.

April sank into a chair at the table. For a moment she considered pursuing the topic of his father, but she decided to let it go. "What are you going to do if we don't find anything tonight?"

Mark sighed and sat down across from her. "I'm not sure." The darkness left his features, and grim determination took its place. "All I know is that somehow I have to get to the bottom of whatever it is Marietta thought was threatening the ranch."

"Then I only hope we find some sort of clue in the last of this paperwork," April said, then opened up the file.

They settled in to read the last group of papers the file contained. For some reason April found concentration more difficult than it had been on the previous night.

She was intensely aware of Mark's scent, an utterly masculine fragrance that heightened her senses. She wondered if her increased awareness of him was due to the fact that Brian wasn't home.

Normally when they worked at the table, Brian was in and out of the room, chattering to Mark or getting an evening snack for himself and Ricky.

Tonight there were no distractions, nothing to divert her attention from Mark's nearness. Was it any wonder she was affected by him? When Derrick had left her, romance with anyone else had been the last thing on her mind.

Left with a mountain of debt and a young son, April had decided she never again wanted a man in her life. From that moment on she'd thrown all her energies into raising Brian and working to rebuild the security that had been stolen.

With her father's death and the realization that once

again her money was gone, as was her home, survival became the name of the game.

For some reason something about Mark reminded her she was more than a working mother. She was a woman. A woman with needs that had been neglected and ignored for a very long time.

Frowning, she once again focused her attention on the papers in front of her. She was here to work on the ranch, get herself and Brian back on their feet financially. She was not here to indulge any fantasies or physical needs with a handsome cowboy.

"Marietta made a lot of notes about the old barn," she commented a few minutes later. She looked up to see Mark eyeing her with interest.

"The old barn? Why would she make any notes about that?"

"It seemed she wanted to check out renovating it and using it for activities. Make it sort of like a community center." April showed him a notation on the paper she had been scanning. In the upper right-hand corner, the word *barn* was written and underlined in bright red ink. "I spoke to your brother about it this morning."

"And what did Matthew say?"

"He said he'd have to discuss the idea with Walter Tilley, but he really didn't think it was a good idea to spend any money renovating, when it wasn't clear how long the ranch would be running."

Mark smiled wryly. "If we lose everything, it won't matter whether the funds were spent or not."

April gazed at him curiously. "What will you do, Mark, if the ranch is sold?"

He leaned back in his chair, the shadows returning

to his eyes. "I don't know. My father always told me I wasn't good for much except working with the stock. If the ranch goes, there'll be no stock to work with."

He sat forward, the shadows once again dissipating beneath a look of grim determination. "The house you came to the other night is mine no matter what. I bought the land from my dad." He waved a hand as if to dismiss the topic. "I can't worry about losing the ranch through defaulting on my father's will until I discover what else might be threatening us. Somebody killed Marietta and almost killed me. That's my number-one concern at the moment."

April frowned thoughtfully and once again stared down at the underlined word on the paper before her. "Barn." It had been written in odd places throughout the file, as if whenever Marietta doodled, the barn had been on her mind.

"That night I happened upon your house, I'd been checking out the old barn," she began. "I know it sounds crazy, but while I was inside I thought I heard a noise."

"What kind of noise?" He leaned even closer to her, his gaze intent.

"I thought it was a voice." She flushed, suddenly embarrassed. "But I'm not sure. It's possible it was just my imagination. I certainly didn't see any indication that anyone was around."

Once again Mark leaned back in his chair, his brow furrowed in thought. "If I was going to run drugs here on the ranch, the old barn would be a perfect place to do it." He stood suddenly. "Feel like a field trip?"

"To the barn?"

He nodded. "I haven't been there in years. Maybe it's time to check it out."

"Is that wise?"

"Billy Carr mentioned a shipment coming in two weeks. That's still over a week away, so we shouldn't encounter any trouble."

"Then what are we going for?" she asked as she stood.

"Because there has to be a sign there, a clue that the barn is being used. If I know where the illegal activity is taking place, then I can eventually figure out who is involved." He grabbed his hat. "Why don't I meet you at your car in five minutes. We'll drive out to the barn and take a quick look around."

Before she had an opportunity to reject or accept his plan, he slipped out the door. This was madness, she told herself as she grabbed her car keys. She was getting too deep into something that absolutely wasn't her business.

Yet, even as she told herself she shouldn't be going, she headed out the door and to her car to await Mark's return.

Someplace in the back of her mind she knew why she was helping him. Because he'd trusted her with his secret, trusted her before his own family. But, more important, she wanted to help him because she liked him, because she somehow thought it was important to him that she believe in him.

Maybe it was the haunted look that filled his eyes when he spoke of his father, the same haunting look that she sometimes saw in her own son's eyes.

She got into her car and put the keys in the ignition,

but didn't start the engine until the passenger door opened and Mark slid in.

"All set," he said, and she started the engine.

"You're going to have to direct me," she said as they pulled away from her cottage. "The night I walked it I had a map. I only got disoriented when I left the barn."

"Don't worry. I'll get us there with no problems," he assured her.

April drove for a moment in silence, concentrating on avoiding ruts and rocks and the occasional cactus. "When Brian and I first arrived here, I thought we'd been sent to hell," she said, breaking the silence.

Mark laughed, a low pleasant chuckle. "That's why the founding fathers named the town Inferno."

She shot him a surreptitious glance. "But you love it here."

He nodded, his gaze directed out the window at the savage landscape. "I do. For me there's a sense of peace, of everlasting endurance that comes from the desert. People change, times change, but this place remains the same and that comforts me." He laughed, as if embarrassed by his words.

But April understood. Over the past several days she'd begun to find the beauty in this place of earth tones and starkness. "I've noticed the sunrises and sunsets are more splendid here than in any place I've ever been," she said.

"Yeah. I think God decided if he wasn't going to give us trees and lakes, he'd give us great sunrises and sunsets, and set the stars so low in the sky it looks like you could just reach up and pluck one and put it in your pocket."

His tone of voice was the same one he used to soothe the horses—gentle, deep and intoxicating. She wanted him to continue talking like that forever. Instead he pointed up ahead. "The barn is just over that rise," he said.

Within minutes the structure came into sight. Weathered and tall, it looked as abandoned as it had the night April had come here by herself.

She parked in front of it, and they got out of the car. "From outward appearances, it doesn't look like anyone's been around here for years," Mark said.

As they moved toward the door, April walked closer to Mark, remembering the sheer panic that had driven her out of the barn before.

The door creaked as he opened it, and the waning evening sun cast its golden light into the interior. Mark stepped in first, April right behind him.

It looked exactly as it had before, from the dust and sand on the floor to the broom standing in the corner. "Where were you when you thought you heard a voice?" he asked.

"I'm not sure.... Standing somewhere there in the center, I think. I'm sure I just imagined it. It's obvious nobody has been here for some time."

"I'm going to check out the loft," he said, and moved toward the stairs.

April waited below, trying to ignore a shiver of apprehension that danced up her spine as he disappeared from her view. She wasn't sure why, but this place gave her the creeps.

She breathed a sigh of relief as Mark came back down the stairs. "Nothing up there," he said. "Just a lot of cobwebs."

A rustling noise came from one of the dark corners. April froze as Mark reached into his boot and pulled out a small pistol. A large lizard raced across the floor. As it headed for the door, it left tiny footprints in the dust.

"You have a gun." April stated the obvious as the lizard disappeared into the evening.

He tucked the gun back into his boot. "I always carry when away from the house. Out here it's common to run into all kinds of varmint."

April didn't even want to think about varmints, either four-legged, six-legged or the most dangerous of all—two-legged. "You ready to go?" she asked, a shiver racing up her spine despite the warmth of the air.

"Yeah, I guess. I don't see anything here that will help me figure things out." Disappointment laced his voice. "Head out that way," he said when they were back in the car, and pointed to the right of where April thought the ranch was. "We'll stop by my place and get something cold to drink before heading back."

They rode in silence for a few minutes. It was April who finally broke the quiet. "I'm sorry, Mark, that you didn't find what you were looking for."

He shrugged. "I was just hoping...I don't know. I'm not even sure I know what I was hoping to find." He sat up straighter in the seat. "But at least now I know whatever is going on isn't going on at the old barn."

"So, by process of elimination, you're one step closer to learning where it's going on."

He laughed, and again April was struck by the utterly pleasant sound. "Are you always so optimistic?"

"Most of the time. Even when Derrick, my ex-husband, left me alone with Brian and a mountain of bills, I didn't lose hope that things would be better." She frowned thoughtfully and parked in front of Mark's house. "It wasn't until my dad's death and the realization that he'd spent everything, that I felt true devastation."

She turned off the car and looked at him. "When Brian and I arrived here, I was pretty defeated. I felt like we were cast out of our previous life without any preparation for a new one."

"And now?"

She smiled. "And now my natural optimism has returned." It was true. In the past week April had once again found her hope—the hope that her future would be brighter, the hope that eventually she'd find a special man who could fill the holes inside her, a man who would want to parent her son, who was so desperate for a father.

"Tell me about your ex-husband," Mark asked.

"I'll trade you one sad story for an icy cold soda," she replied.

He grinned. "Deal."

Together they got out of the car and walked to the house. Mark unlocked the front door and led her through the attractive living room to the kitchen. She sat at the table while he grabbed two sodas from the refrigerator, then he joined her.

He popped the top of her can, handed it to her, then eyed her expectantly.

"I had just turned eighteen when I met Derrick,"

she began. "He was twenty-two and I thought he was the most handsome, charming, together man I'd ever met." April sighed as her memories pulled her back in time. "My mother had just passed away, and I was reeling with the loss. Derrick filled me with dreams of a wonderful future together."

She shook her head with a rueful smile. "If there's one thing Derrick could do very well, it was dream. Unfortunately, the dreams were rarely followed up with anything that remotely resembled work."

"You didn't know that when you married him?" Mark's soft voice pulled her from the past.

"No. We dated for three months, then I discovered I was pregnant. We married and, with a little nest egg I'd saved, managed to buy a small house complete with a white picket fence."

"Ah, the old picket fence trick."

She smiled, recognizing he was attempting to keep her memories, her foray into the past, painless. "Yeah, that picket fence gets to women every time." She paused to take a drink of her soda. "The long and short of it is that Derrick always had a get-rich-quick scheme. I worked and saved money, and he dreamed and spent what little I could save. By the time our marriage ended, we'd lost the house, we had massive credit-card debt, and Derrick had disappeared."

"And you never heard from him again?"

"Up until the time of my father's death a month ago, Derrick would call occasionally." She frowned and her hand tightened around the soda can. "He'd call to ask to borrow money, but he'd never ask to speak with Brian. With each of those phone calls, any pain I'd felt over the demise of my marriage left me.''

A small, self-conscious laugh escaped her. ''Anyway, that's my story. After Derrick, Brian and I moved in with my father. I worked at a hotel as a social director, and Dad watched Brian for me. I thought I was finally getting back on my feet, until I discovered that Dad had lost everything.'' She winced and offered Mark a small smile. ''I seem to have a habit of trusting the wrong men in my life.''

To her surprise he reached across the table and covered her hand with his. Warmth swept up her arm. His hand was big enough to completely engulf hers, and she could feel the calluses that spoke of hard labor—calluses that only added to the tactile pleasure of his hand over hers.

''I'm sorry you've had a rough time.'' His voice was soft as a whisper in her ear, as potent as a caress across her bare flesh.

With a flush of heat rising through her, she pulled her hand away and stood. ''Why don't you give me a tour of your house? You mentioned the other night that you built it yourself.'' The pitch of her voice sounded higher than normal to her own ears.

''Okay,'' he agreed and stood, a lazy smile playing at the corners of his mouth. The smile told her he knew what had caused her slight breathlessness, the higher pitch to her voice.

Desire.

He led her through the living room and down a hallway. ''We'll start the tour back here,'' he said as he opened a door to reveal an empty spare room. ''I built the house five years ago.''

He opened the next door in the hallway to show her what appeared to be another spare bedroom, although this one held a double bed and a dresser. Next was a bathroom. "I was engaged and thought this was going to be a home for me and my wife and our family."

April looked at him in surprise. "What happened?"

He frowned as he led her to the last doorway. "She broke it off." He smiled wryly. "I forgot to build a picket fence. She found somebody else who had one." He opened up the last door to reveal what was obviously the master bedroom.

"Oh, Mark. What a wonderful view." April walked across the thick, plush carpeting to the wall of floor-to-ceiling windows and the French door that led out to a rock and cactus garden.

As she looked out to where the sun was just giving a final kiss of color to the sky, she was aware of Mark coming to stand behind her.

She was also acutely aware of the king-size bed. As she'd passed it to get to the windows, she'd noticed the blue bedspread with narrow cranberry stripes. Bold. Masculine.

Like Mark.

"This is my favorite time of day to be here in this room." His voice was once again that soft, deep lull that made her want to close her eyes and fall into him.

She knew she should move away from him the moment he placed his hands on her shoulders. But she couldn't move. She was trapped by the need she felt flowing from him. And if she were perfectly honest with herself, she'd admit that she was captive to her own need, as well.

She turned to him and saw the colors of the sunset reflected in his eyes, flames of desire that danced amid the steel-gray flecks.

"April." He whispered her name in the instant before his lips claimed hers.

Any thought she had of moving, of stepping away from him, banished beneath the fire of his kiss. His arms wound around her, pulling her tight against him, and in the hardness of his body she recognized the extent of his need.

He deepened the kiss, his tongue lightly touching first her lower lip, then delving into her mouth to battle with her own.

April raised her hands, skimming upward over the bulge of his biceps, across the expanse of his shoulders, and locked her fingers at the nape of his neck.

His kiss stole all thought from her mind, weakened her knees with its intensity and lit a hunger deep inside her that ached to be fulfilled.

When he finally raised his mouth from hers, she again told herself to step away from him. But her body refused to leave the warmth and thrill of his arms.

"April, I want you." The yearning in his voice stirred her more deeply than anything else she had ever heard. His gaze held hers intently, and she knew he waited for her answer.

She also knew she could tell him no, halt the insanity at this very moment and there would be no hard feelings, no negative repercussions. She could walk away from this moment and this man and spend the rest of her life regretting it.

Why not? A little voice whispered as she caught a glimpse of the massive bed. Why not give in to temptation and just enjoy being a woman with this man? She had absolutely nothing he could take from her. Her money was gone, her home sold, her pitiful possessions not worth anything.

She had nothing more to lose to any man.

Decision made, she smiled at him, a tremulous smile, as she stepped out of his arms and walked to the side of the bed.

His eyes flared hot and hungry as she sank down onto the bedspread and beckoned him to join her. "Are you sure?" he asked, his voice husky. "I'm not offering a picket fence."

"I'm not asking for one," she replied. "Just right now...that's all I want."

Apparently it was exactly the reply he was waiting for.

Before she could catch her breath, he joined her on the bed and pulled her against him for a kiss more fiery than the last.

Chapter 9

When Mark had suggested they stop by the house for something cold to drink, there had been no thought of seduction on his mind.

But the moment he'd seen her standing at his bedroom windows with the golden hues of dusk cascading over her, his desire to take her, possess her, had suddenly raged out of control.

Now his mouth claimed hers with fierce hunger as he pulled her closer against him. She fit perfectly, her breasts pressed into his chest and her long legs against his.

As he deepened the kiss with his tongue, his fingers worked the buttons of her blouse. He realized someplace in the back of his mind that he'd wanted her from the first time he'd seen her.

She'd stood on their front porch, looking so achingly vulnerable and something about her, in that first moment of meeting her and every moment since, had drawn him.

He knew she'd been drawn to him, as well. He'd recognized her attraction, seen it in her features, felt it pulse in the air between them.

The past three nights of working at her kitchen table, sitting next to her, had been an exquisite form of torture. He'd left her cottage each night with the scent of her whirling dizzily in his head, creating a tension in him that threatened to explode.

As he unfastened the last button on her blouse, he broke his kiss and gazed down at her, giving her a final opportunity to halt what had begun.

Her eyes were as he'd imagined they would be, the deep green of summer heat. Her lips were swollen from his kiss, and her breathing was rapid. Her beauty ached inside him, and he wanted more...all of her. But he didn't want to take what she didn't want to give.

She apparently sensed his hesitation. She parted her unbuttoned blouse, exposing to his heated gaze a pale pink lacy bra and the full thrust of her breasts beneath.

The simple gesture was all the acquiescence he needed. With a groan, he splayed his hands over her bra, and his mouth sought hers once again.

Her nipples hardened beneath his hands, pressing up taut against the lace bra. Mark's heart beat frantically as she moved her hands beneath his shirt, her fingers dancing up the bare skin of his back.

Mark quickly grew impatient with the clothing that still separated them. He sat up and pulled his shirt over his head. Aware of her gaze on him, he stood next to the bed and removed his boots.

He placed the pistol on the floor next to the bed, then took off his jeans, leaving himself clad only in a pair of briefs that in no way could hide his intense desire.

He pulled her to a sitting position, then gently pushed the blouse from her shoulders, allowing it to fall from her body and to the bed behind her.

He didn't speak, nor did she. The only sounds in the room was the whisper of material as it was removed and their rapid breathing.

As he reached behind her to unclasp her bra, he pressed his lips against the side of her neck, savoring the soft, scented skin. She gasped in pleasure and tilted her head back, allowing him further access to her neck and throat.

The bra fell away, exposing her bare breasts to his hungry gaze. He covered them with his hands, her nipples pebble hard against his palm. She moaned, and the sound of her pleasure shot fire through his veins.

As he moved his mouth to where his hands had been, she tangled her hands in his hair, her breath coming in tiny pants and sighs.

Gently he leaned her back on the bed, so she was again stretched out. His fingers trembled as he worked to unfasten her jeans. When he got them undone, she helped him remove them by lifting her hips.

Only her pale pink panties and his briefs separated them now. Mark moved so his lower body was on top of hers. She welcomed him, parting her legs to allow him to nestle as close as possible.

Even with the material that kept them from complete intimate contact, he could feel the heat that radiated from her very center. It was a heat that beckoned him, forced the blood to surge through him, and he struggled to maintain control.

Mark had known instinctively that April had a well of passion inside her. He'd seen flashes of it in her eyes whenever he'd touched her. Now that passion was unleashed. She met his kisses with a hunger of her own, met him caress for caress, stroke for stroke as their foreplay lingered.

Her fingers danced across the expanse of his back, warm and teasing. At the same time her hips moved beneath his. At first her movement was tentative, almost imperceptible.

Mark shifted slightly so he was pressed against her heat. It was an exquisite form of torture, to be so close to possessing her, yet stymied by the thin material of underclothes.

April gasped as he met her hip thrust. At the same time he lowered his head to capture the peak of her breast with his mouth. He could feel her heartbeat thundering with pleasure and knew the rhythm of her heart matched his own.

It didn't take long before he had to banish the last of the barriers that separated them. He needed complete possession, wanted to own her for this moment.

He rolled off her, pleasure winging through him as she moaned in abandonment. He quickly turned her moan of displeasure to one of satisfaction as he eased her panties down and off.

The light in the room had nearly extinguished with the coming of night, leaving the room in the dusky purple of deep twilight. And it was in this surreal illumination that Mark gazed at April, taking in the lines and curves of her nakedness.

''You are so beautiful,'' he whispered. It was true. She wasn't model thin. She was lush and rounded and all the things a woman should be.

He saw the shiver that worked through her—recognized it wasn't the temperature of the room that caused it, but rather his words—and the intense desire that shone from her eyes. Their green depths beckoned him into the heat she offered.

He took off his briefs and once again covered her body with his own. As his mouth covered hers, he slowly eased himself into her.

She welcomed him, her arms wrapping around him to pull him closer...closer still. He was aware of a racing heartbeat, but couldn't discern if it was hers or his own.

For a long moment he didn't move, couldn't move for fear of completely losing control. She surrounded him with moist heat.

He knew if he moved, it would be the beginning of the end. And he didn't want it to end. Not yet. He hadn't had nearly enough of her sweet lips, her heady scent or her soft skin.

As much as he didn't want to move, his body had a mind of its own. Despite any desire to the contrary, his hips moved without volition, thrusting rhythmically against hers.

She met him thrust for thrust, hands clutching, fingers raking across his back. Moans of pleasure escaped her and fed his exhilaration. As they moved faster and faster together, Mark gave himself over completely to the sweet summer heat of April.

"You okay?" he asked moments later as they lingered side by side on the bed. He could just make out her features in the soft moonlight that drifted in the window.

"Sure." She propped herself up on one elbow facing him. "It's just been a long time for me. I'm not sure I remember how to make small talk after sex."

He smiled, finding her candor refreshing. "I'm just grateful you didn't decide to try to small talk *during* sex."

She laughed, a wonderfully sexy sound. "I couldn't think, let alone small talk." She reached out and touched his cheek.

He grabbed her hand and kissed her palm. For a moment he wished they could remain here forever. No ranch, no murder, no world outside of the bed that held the two of them.

"This is nice," she said. "But I should get back." Still she made no effort to move, as if she were reluctant to release the moment.

He pulled her close to him and for a few minutes simply held her in the moonlight that spilled into the window. He wondered what it would be like to sleep like this every night, with the warmth of a woman in his arms...with the warmth of April in his arms.

"I should get back," she repeated. This time she left his arms, scooted off the bed, grabbed her clothes and disappeared into the bathroom.

Mark rolled over on his back and stared unseeing at the ceiling. Somehow the simple touch of her hand to his cheek had almost seemed more intimate than the lovemaking they'd just shared.

The directions of his thoughts as he'd held her had been frightening. What kind of fool was he to imagine that he could be enough for a woman like April? That he could make her happy for a lifetime? Foolish thoughts.

He frowned, hoping he hadn't just made an enormous mistake. He liked April, liked her a lot. But she deserved somebody who could give her things he couldn't. If he gave her the opportunity, eventually she'd find him lacking, as Rachel had. He didn't intend to give her the chance.

He rolled off the bed and grabbed his clothes. By the time he was dressed, she was out of the bathroom. Together they left the house. "You can drive back," she said as she handed him the keys to her car. "I don't trust my sense of direction in the dark."

Again Mark had the feeling that somehow a transition had occurred between them. In the act of handing over the keys to her car, she'd indicated a new sense of trust in him.

They rode in silence for a moment. "What was she like?" April broke the silence.

Mark didn't need to ask whom she was speaking of. "Then or now?" he asked.

"Either...both."

Mark thought of the woman he'd once believed he would marry. "Rachel was a nice woman...still is. Her father was friends with mine. It was my father's idea that we date."

"Your father liked her?"

Mark tightened his grip on the steering wheel. "My

father wanted heirs for the ranch. He thought Rachel would be a good mother.'' In actuality, what Adam had said was that Rachel had the wide hips that would probably make her a good brood mare.

He struggled to loosen his grasp on the steering wheel despite the tension that suddenly assailed him. ''My father wanted grandsons and I was the chosen one to continue the Delaney line. Matthew was too important to the ranch to waste himself being a husband and father. Luke was too young and too wild to fulfill that particular duty.''

''And so you were to be the sacrificial lamb, so to speak.''

''Yeah, although at the time it didn't seem like such a terrible way to sacrifice myself.'' He offered her a wry grin. ''Far better than having to fling myself into the mouth of an active volcano.''

''So, what happened?''

Mark focused his attention out the window and reached back into his past to retrieve bits of memory. ''Nothing earth-shattering. Rachel and I dated, began planning our wedding and I started work on this house. As the house went up, I realized Rachel seemed to be distancing herself from me. Finally, a month before the wedding, she told me she couldn't go through with it, that she just didn't love me.''

He didn't share with April all the reasons Rachel had listed. A litany of sins for which Mark had no answer.

''Were you devastated?''

He thought for a moment before replying. ''At first I was. Then I realized I was more upset about ruining my father's plans than I was about losing Rachel.''

"Where is she now?"

"Married to Samuel Rogers who owns the ranch next to ours. She's the mother of two and seems genuinely happy. I'm glad for her. She deserves to be happy."

"And what about you?"

"Me? I'm grateful the entire experience happened. It made me realize I'm not cut out to be a husband. Marriage is definitely not in my future."

He was grateful to see the lights of the ranch just ahead, because he was suddenly irritated by her questions, questions that were making him remember his own inadequacies.

He'd allowed her the intimacy of his body, but that didn't mean he owed her the intimacy of his mind. "What is this, twenty questions?" he snapped suddenly.

She stiffened her shoulders. "I'm sorry. I didn't mean to pry."

But he knew that was exactly what she meant to do. And it scared him. He didn't want her to think that what they'd just shared implied promise, held the hope of any future.

"Mark, I don't want you to think that tonight changes anything."

He stopped the car in front of her cottage and turned to her in surprise. Apparently she'd been thinking the same things he had.

"You don't have to worry that because we slept together I now have expectations of a relationship. I don't." She opened her car door, and in the light that blinked on overhead he saw the blush that stained her cheeks.

She held out her hand for her keys, and he handed them to her. "Mark, I like having you as a friend, but I'm certainly not looking for a relationship. I've had enough men in my life to last me a lifetime." Her blush intensified. "The sex was great, but that's all it was." She got out of the car and closed the door.

Mark quickly followed, somehow feeling like a heel.

"April." He caught up with her as she was unlocking her front door. She turned to him, her face achingly beautiful in the silvery moonlight. The need to apologize was quickly overwhelmed by the greater need to capture her lips with his.

And he did just that, capturing her lips with his. She briefly accepted his kiss, then stepped away from him. "Good night, Mark."

"I'll see you tomorrow," he said, but before he could say anything else she slipped through the door and was gone.

He stood for a long moment on her porch, staring up at the moon overhead and trying to work through the conflicting emotions that raced through him. She'd said everything he'd wanted to hear. He should be feeling at ease.

And yet, the casual way she'd dismissed their lovemaking as simple sex bothered him. He scoffed inwardly at himself and stepped off her porch.

Heading back to the main house, he told himself things were just as they should be with April. He should be feeling just fine. After all, she expected nothing from him and that was exactly what he could give her. Because he was Mark Delaney...because he was his father's son.

* * *

April didn't see him the next day. She looked for him around seven that evening, when he usually showed up to go through Marietta's files. But he didn't appear.

She sat at the table alone and opened the file. There weren't many pages left that they hadn't gone over. She would look them over alone.

Over the next hour she tried to concentrate on the paperwork, but her mind kept skipping back to the night before.

Making love with Mark had been every bit as breathtaking as she'd fantasized it would be. He'd been alternatively demanding and gentle, commanding and vulnerable, taking and giving.

She'd awakened that morning with her body aching, but it was the pleasant ache of a woman who'd been fully loved.

Not loved, she reminded herself. What they'd shared had nothing to do with love and everything to do with an explosion of lust. Chemistry had been at work between them from the moment they'd met. Last night they had acted upon that chemistry. Nothing more. Nothing less.

At least this time she understood the rules going into it. Unlike Derrick, who had crept into her heart like a thief, stolen all that she had to give, then left her bereft and broken.

She wouldn't, couldn't give Mark that same power over her. She knew exactly where he stood. And she knew she'd be a fool to trust again, especially a man who had begun a relationship with her based on deception.

However, she had lied to him. When she'd told him the last thing she wanted was another man in her life, it had been a lie. She'd sensed Mark's distance, felt his panic when he'd thought she was getting too close, asking questions that went to his heart.

She'd said what she had—about them sharing good sex and her wanting nothing more from him—to ease his conscience. He'd made it more than clear that he had no intention of pursuing a real relationship with her, one that would eventually lead to a lifetime commitment.

She didn't know what sort of baggage Mark carried from his father, but it seemed to be plentiful. She didn't understand the Delaney family dynamics and she wasn't in a position to fix them.

All she knew for certain was that when she found the man who would be her true soul mate and a stepfather to Brian, he would want a future with her as much as she did with him. And it seemed obvious that man wasn't Mark Delaney.

The next week flew by. The ranch hummed with activity as the hired help worked to ready things for the arriving guests. Both Brian and April received their first paychecks and celebrated by opening savings accounts and eating dinner in town.

Throughout the week April saw Mark often. She saw him in the corral working the horses, bumped into him in the main house as she came out of a meeting with Johnna. Each morning after working several hours in the stables, Brian came in chattering about what Mark said or what Mark did.

April only knew the things Mark didn't do. He

didn't come by the cottage to see her. He nodded to her, smiled at her, but gave no indication that she was anything other than a fellow worker.

April told herself it was ridiculous to feel hurt. She'd told him she expected nothing from him, and she'd meant it. But at night in her lonely bed, she remembered those moments of being held in his arms, of his mouth taking such utter possession of hers, and she realized she wanted him again.

It had nothing to do with love, she told herself again and again. It was about need, about want. It was all about hormones not hearts. She would never, ever allow her heart to be vulnerable again.

At the moment she had little thought for Mark. She stood before her bedroom mirror, applying the last of her makeup. Her mind raced, going over all the details of the welcoming barbecue she'd arranged for the guests who had arrived that day.

She was unbelievably nervous about the event. She desperately hoped everything went smoothly, that the guests had a roaring good time and she'd finally get a nod of approval from Mr. Stuffy, Matthew Delaney.

She stepped back to view her reflection. The denim dress she wore wasn't new, but had only been worn once before. Sleeveless, it exposed the tan she'd acquired over the past couple of days and hugged her curves in all the right places.

"Mom." Brian knocked on her door. "Isn't it time yet?"

She opened the door and smiled. "Yes, it's time for us to get to the barbecue. But you know it doesn't really start for another hour."

"I know, but you said there's lots of work to do."

Brian grabbed his cowboy hat and plopped it on his head, his smile eager. "I told Ricky to come early, too. He can help with the work."

"Many hands make light work," April said as they left the cottage.

Directly in front of the main house a flurry of activity was taking place. Several of the cowboys were busy setting up chairs, and a band was unpacking its equipment. The scent of savory ribs and tangy sauce wafted in the air from the industrial-size steel cooker. Baked beans bubbled in large pots over fire pits, and April knew there were tons of potato salad in the refrigerator, just waiting to be served.

With Brian's help, she busied herself setting up tables, placing them close enough together to inspire friendly chatter.

By the time they'd set up the tables, Ricky had arrived, and April assigned the two boys to the task of arranging name tags on one of the tables.

Feeling as if everything was under control, she walked over to the cooker to take a peek at the ribs. The man wielding tongs and basting brush didn't need a name tag. His strong features and dark hair identified him distinctly as a Delaney.

"You must be Luke," she said. "I'm April, the new social director."

"Ah, yes, the lovely April. Mark has mentioned you about a hundred times." He gestured with his tongs to the surrounding commotion. "I assume you're the cause for all of this."

She nodded. "Guilty as charged."

He grinned, and instantly she understood why Luke Delaney might have a reputation with the women.

Handsome as the devil, he had a wicked gleam in his eyes, as if he had the ability to see beneath your clothing. Mark's attractiveness was far less blatant, and to April, far more appealing.

"Actually, it's a good idea," he said, then smiled dryly. "We'll see if the ranch stays open long enough to repeat the festivities."

"We all have our fingers crossed," April said.

She said her goodbyes to Luke, then went back to check on Brian and Ricky's progress with the name tags. None of the Delaneys seemed to have much hope of holding things together and maintaining control of the ranch.

What would happen to Mark if the ranch was lost? He, more than any of the others, seemed most vulnerable to the loss of the place.

Not my problem, she told herself firmly. Then, realizing the first of the guests had begun to arrive, she hurried to greet them.

Nearly two hours later she sank down at one of the tables, exhausted but pleased as she watched the people dancing to the boot-kicking country music. Children chased one another, playing games of tag amid the grown-ups.

April's crowning moment had occurred ten minutes before when Matthew passed her with a "good job" and the hint of a smile.

"Why aren't you dancing?"

April tried to ignore the pleasure that swept through her at Mark's voice near her ear. He walked around her chair to stand in front of her.

"Nobody has asked me," she replied.

He held out a hand to her. "I'm asking."

She wanted to say no, to tell him to find somebody else to dance with, to hold in his arms. But she didn't have the willpower. He looked too handsome in his tight jeans and short-sleeved Western shirt. His dark hair was in careless disarray, only intensifying his overwhelming attractiveness.

With a sigh, she stood and allowed him to pull her closer to the band. "I've missed you this week," he said as they began to two-step with the other couples.

She looked at him in surprise. "Missed me?" she echoed faintly.

He nodded. "It's been a hell of a week. I spent a lot of my time in town, staking out Larry Greco's place, hoping to find out what he's up to and what it has to do with the ranch."

She watched as frustration etched a line across his forehead.

"I've also staked out the old barn every night this week, but haven't seen anything or anyone. And I still don't know what the supposed shipment is all about."

Instinctively April's arm tightened around him. "I wish you'd stop this Lone Ranger stuff and go to the sheriff," she said.

He grinned at her, a lazy, sexy grin that caused her heart to skip a beat. "You worried about me?" he asked.

She eyed him seriously. "Yes." And in that instant, she realized she did care about Mark—more than as a co-worker, more than as a friend. Her emotions where he was concerned went far beyond that depth. The realization both thrilled her and frightened her.

She looked away from him, not wanting him to see

any emotion in her eyes, any telltale sign of affection. "I'd worry about anyone taking the kinds of risks you are," she said briskly.

He tightened his arms around her and for a moment she closed her eyes and pretended it meant something, something more than lust, something more than sheer physical attraction.

"Hey, Mark, buddy." Billy Carr slapped a hand on Mark's back. "How about I cut in and take the little lady for a twirl."

Mark grinned one of his patented empty smiles at Billy. "She doesn't want to twirl. She wants to dance, and I'm dancing with her."

"Yeah, well, maybe she'd rather dance with a man who isn't one taco shy of a combination plate," Billy said, then laughed as if he'd said something incredibly witty.

"Actually, I hate tacos, but I love dancing with Mark," April said coolly, satisfied when Billy's smile instantly fell.

"When I'm able to reclaim my intelligence, the first thing I'm going to do is fire his ass," Mark said as Billy stalked away.

"Does he say things like that often?"

"All the time." He offered her a wry grin. "If you want to learn the true character of people, just act like you're mentally challenged. It brings out the worst and the best in people."

"But you're betraying the people closest to you with this act," April protested.

His eyes darkened, became tormented. "You mean my family? I can't forget what Marietta said, April. I can't forget that it's possible my family is intimately involved in whatever the hell is going on here.''

She was teetering on the verge of falling in love with Mark Delaney. The realization struck her with the force of a lightning bolt. And it came at an odd time, right there on the dance floor in the midst of a budding argument.

April walked back to the table and sat down once again, afraid her legs wouldn't hold her as she faced the truth that sang in her heart.

Loving Mark would be a ridiculously foolish thing to do and yet she didn't know how to stop her heart from feeling for him, caring about him, worrying about him…loving him.

She rubbed her forehead, wondering what kind of weakness she possessed, what character flaw it was that made her vulnerable to loving the wrong men. How on earth could she possibly be falling in love with a man who was proving himself quite adept at deceiving his entire family?

Chapter 10

Mark had never been so frustrated in his life. And the frustration seemed to batter him from all sides. He was tired of playing the fool. Forcing the empty smile was becoming more and more difficult. Pretending not to understand the events going on around him was becoming torturous.

Sheriff Broder had not returned with any more questions, and Mark had spent hours agonizing over whether he should go and talk to the sheriff about what little he knew. Broder's investigation appeared to be stymied, and Mark's personal investigation was just as dead.

He'd spent an entire week hidden by the cloak of night, watching the old barn and hoping to discover what Marietta had apparently known. Nothing had happened. The barn had remained empty and dark, and Mark's frustration had grown by leaps and bounds.

Twice in the past week Johnna had threatened to walk away from the ranch and the will. It had taken talks from both Matthew and Mark to convince her to give the arrangement more time.

It wasn't just the mystery and the uncertainty of the ranch's future that filled him with frustration. It was also April. April with her halo hair and winsome green eyes. The week he'd spent away from her had been a torment.

He'd gotten accustomed to spending time at her place in the evenings, small talking as they went over Marietta's file. He'd made a conscious decision to stay away, but it had been the most difficult thing he'd ever done.

But he'd wanted to make sure she understood their lovemaking had changed nothing between them. Unfortunately, things had changed for him, and the week away from her had only underscored the changes.

He missed her smiles and her low, sexy laughter. He missed the way her eyes warmed and sparkled as she spoke of her son, how they darkened and grew luminous when she talked about her past.

He wanted her again, wanted her with every fiber of his being. And he didn't just want her body. He didn't just want her kisses and her caresses. He wanted her smiles and her laughter. He wanted her memories and her disappointments, her successes and her dreams.

But he didn't want her love. And he absolutely refused to consider loving her. The Delaneys weren't good at love, and Mark refused to put himself in the position of letting down another woman.

Still, that didn't stop him from seeking her out. It

was early evening when he left the main house and walked toward her cottage, hungry to spend some time in her company.

The past three days had been busy ones as nearly all the guests had been eager to ride, and he'd spent most of those days saddling horses and leading trail rides.

Tonight the ranch was quiet. The town of Inferno was having an ice-cream social and most of the guests had gone to it. April's car was parked out in front of her cottage, so he knew she hadn't gone into town.

He knocked on her door, a rush of anticipation sweeping through him. When she opened the door, her eyes widened in surprise. "Mark," she said, and there was pleasure in her voice, a pleasure that pulled an evocative joy through him.

"Hi. Things are quiet around the old homestead, so I thought I'd drop by for a visit."

"Come in." She stepped aside to allow him entry.

Instantly he saw that the room had been transformed by personal touches and items of hers. An eight-by-ten framed photo of her and Brian now graced the space where an old landscape print had been. Rose-colored throw pillows had been added to the sofa, along with a like-colored silk floral arrangement in the center of the coffee table.

"You've added things," he said.

She nodded. "I wasn't going to, but Brian insisted." She gestured him toward the sofa. "I think he needed our things filling the room in order to give him a sense of permanence, no matter how false it might be."

"So, you know things have been shaky the past week." He sat on the sofa.

She nodded and joined him on the opposite end of the sofa. "Matthew set me up sharing an office in the house with Walter Tilley. Walter mentioned that Johnna was talking about forgetting the terms of the will."

Mark frowned. "Walter shouldn't be discussing family business outside of the family."

"I don't think he meant any harm." April hurried to the small, dapper man's defense.

Mark sighed. "I know you're right. Walter's a good man." He raked a hand through his hair, then leaned back and eyed her curiously. "If the ranch is sold, what will you and Brian do?"

She leaned back, as well. The rose-colored pillows behind her appeared to pull a becoming color to her cheeks. "I don't know. I know I won't go back to Tulsa." She frowned. "I'll probably try to find a position with a hotel. Maybe Tucson. I hear there's work there."

"Brian will be disappointed if you have to leave here," Mark said. "Speaking of Brian, where is he?"

She pointed to the closed bedroom door. "I took him to the library yesterday and he checked out a bunch of books about cowboys. He's been poring over them ever since."

Mark smiled, thinking of the young boy. "He grills me about cowboys every morning when we're working together in the stables."

"Brian is convinced that cowboys are the heroes of the world." She rubbed her forehead, as if a headache were bothering her. Mark fought the impulse to reach out and rub it for her. "He thinks cowboys are all good men, men who would never leave their wives and children."

"Well, you know that's a fantasy. Cowboys are just like any other men. There are good ones and bad ones."

She stopped rubbing her forehead and eyed him curiously. "And which kind are you, Mark Delaney? A good cowboy or a bad one?"

His initial instinct was to whip off a humorous reply, but the seriousness in her tone and the intensity of her gaze stopped him. He thought for a moment. He wanted to say he was one of the good cowboys, but the thoughts he was entertaining about her at that very moment were distinctly disreputable.

Before he could reply, Brian came out of his bedroom. "Mark!" His face lit with pleasure. "I didn't hear you come in." He plopped down between Mark and April on the sofa.

"Your mom says you've been reading up about cowboys," Mark said.

Brian nodded. "I got a whole bunch of books from the library. Can you read, Mark?" It was an innocent question from an innocent child, but it pointed directly to the deception Mark had been living for more than a month.

"Sure," he replied.

"You know how to play cards?" Brian asked.

"What kind of cards?"

"Poker." Brian leaned toward him eagerly. "Cowboys play poker." He looked from Mark to his mother, then back again. "Why don't the three of us play some poker right now?"

"Brian, honey, I'm sure Mark isn't interested in—"

"Sounds like fun to me," Mark interrupted April with a wink. "We cowboys never turn down a hot game of poker."

"I'll go get a deck of cards." Brian jumped off the sofa and raced for his room.

"You don't have to do this," April said as she and Mark moved from the sofa to the small table.

"I know that. I wanted to." He grinned. "And I think you and I should make a little side wager."

She eyed him suspiciously. "What kind of a side wager?"

"The winner gets to kiss the loser."

She laughed in protest. It was that low, sexy laugh that made him want to sweep her into his arms and make love to her right then and there.

"What's the matter?" he teased. "Scared of a little kiss?"

"Of course not," she replied, her cheeks flushing with color. "You're on," she said just as Brian flew back into the room.

They played for toothpicks, and it didn't take Mark long to realize several things. Brian never bluffed. If he bet, he usually had a winning hand.

April liked to bluff, but each time before she did, she toyed with a strand of her hair, unconsciously letting Mark know she was misleading him. She also played to win, her eyes flashing with a competitiveness he found charming.

For Mark, it was an evening unlike any he'd ever experienced. The warmth of love that existed between Brian and April seemed to spill over on him. The shared laughter felt good, and he realized this was what family felt like—warmth, laughter, good times.

He reached back in his memories for one single time he'd experienced the same kind of feelings with his own family. There were none.

You can make memories for yourself, a small voice whispered inside him. You can make memories with this woman and this needy boy. You could build a family with them and fill the hunger inside you.

He mentally shook his head to still the voice that whispered of forgotten dreams and fantasies. It had been those kinds of foolish dreams that had led him into his relationship with Rachel. But she had seen through the fantasy and recognized that Mark didn't have the qualities it took to be a husband and a father.

But that didn't mean he couldn't enjoy this night of shared laughter and warmth with Brian and April. That didn't mean he wasn't fighting overwhelming desire for April.

The desire that raged inside him was fed by his thigh brushing April's beneath the table, their hands meeting over the cards. Her smile seared heat through him, and the memory of their lovemaking stoked the flames even higher.

They played for a couple of hours, then took a break so April could make popcorn. Mark used the opportunity to step outside and stretch in an attempt to alleviate some of the tension that tightened his muscles.

Brian walked out with him and mimicked Mark's movements, stretching with arms overhead. ''Nice night,'' he commented.

Mark hid a smile at Brian's attempt to make adult small talk. "Sure is," he agreed.

"You think my mom is pretty?"

Mark looked at the young boy with surprise. "Sure, she's real pretty."

Brian nodded, as if satisfied. "She's a real good cook, too. And sometimes when I'm sick, she rubs my back and she has really soft, nice hands."

Mark knew intimately the qualities of April's hands...how her fingers could dance over heated flesh, how they grasped his shoulders when he'd taken her.

"Hey, guys," April called from the doorway, "popcorn is ready."

The scent of the buttery snack drew him inside. As they resumed their card playing, Mark tried to ignore the craving April stirred in him. But he couldn't.

And he knew she felt it, too. Physical awareness spun in the air between them, a shimmering thread of want that connected them on an ethereal level.

He could tell she felt it, in the way she pulled her hand back too quickly when they touched and the way she averted her gaze from his.

At midnight they called a halt to the game. Brian's eyelids were drooping, and it was obvious it was past his bedtime.

"This was fun," Brian said as he got up from the table. He walked to where Mark still sat and in a surprising gesture threw his arms around Mark's neck. "Thanks, Mark." He hurried to his bedroom, as if embarrassed by his spontaneous display of affection.

Mark picked up the cards as April tucked her son

into bed. Brian's hug had unsettled Mark, opening his heart in a way that it had not been before.

He remembered the brief conversation they'd had outside, when Brian listed April's attributes in an obvious matchmaking attempt. The last thing Mark wanted to do was fall into Brian's fantasy, play to the boy's need for a father.

He stood as April reentered the living room. "Guess I'd better get out of here," he said. "Morning comes early."

She stepped outside with him. The warm night air wrapped around them, and the stars winked down from the black velvet sky.

"It was fun, Mark." Her voice was soft, and she stood close enough to him that her floral scent teased him.

"Yeah, it was," he agreed. He shoved his hands into his pockets and stepped off the porch.

"Aren't you going to collect on your bet?"

He turned to look at her, intending to laugh off the silly bet. But any laughter that might have surfaced died as desire welled up inside him.

There was an aching vulnerability in her eyes, a sweet acceptance of whatever he chose to give her, or whatever he chose to withhold.

He pulled his hands from his pockets and rejoined her on the porch, unable to fight what felt so inevitable. Before he even reached for her, she tilted her face upward in anticipation of their kiss.

Wrapping his arms around her, he pulled her tight to him, the desire he'd fought all evening now wild and running through his veins. Her mouth opened beneath his, welcoming him.

An eternity seemed to pass before he finally broke the kiss, breathless and hungry for more. The intensity of his hunger shocked him. He'd thought that making love to her that first and only time would be enough to satisfy him. But that initial experience had only stirred a deeper, more profound hunger inside him.

He dropped his arms from around her and swallowed hard, fighting to control his need for her. He didn't want to need her. He didn't want to need anyone.

"I'll see you later," he said, then turned and walked away, mentally running as fast as he could to escape his own disturbing emotions.

April remained on her porch for several long minutes, drawing in deep breaths of air in an attempt to ease the tension that coiled tightly inside her.

Mark's kiss had stirred longing—the longing to once again be held in his arms, to feel his naked body against her own. Her entire being ached with the memory of making love with him, and she wanted it to happen again and again and again.

She sank down on the stoop and tilted her head back so she had a panoramic view of the sky overhead. It was impossible to blame her feelings on a coyote moon. That phase had passed and now only half a moon was apparent in the sky.

For so long, the sum total of her self-identity had been as a mother and caregiver. Now Mark made her feel vibrantly alive as a desirable woman. She'd almost forgotten how wonderfully compelling that could feel.

But, beyond the obvious sexual attraction, what did

he feel for her? He didn't see himself as a husband or a father. So, what was she doing with him? Was she once again falling in love with the wrong kind of man? A man who couldn't possibly give her what she desired—a future of happiness together?

With a weary sigh, she stood and went back into the cottage. She didn't know the answers. She only knew she felt powerless to fight her feelings for Mark.

"Mom?" Brian called to her as she started into her bedroom.

She went into his room and sat on the edge of his bed. "What are you doing still awake?" She reached out and pushed a strand of his hair from his forehead.

"I was just thinking."

"Thinking about what?"

Brian leaned up and bunched the pillow behind him so he was sitting up a little. "Mark seemed smarter tonight, didn't he?"

April grinned. "You just think he was smarter because he beat both of us at poker."

Brian didn't return her smile. Instead his forehead wrinkled with thought. "I'm being serious, Mom. Ricky's mom told me about Mark getting hurt and that his brain doesn't work exactly right anymore. But I think it works just fine. Don't you?"

April's smile fell away as she realized the tangle of lies Mark had spun to perpetuate his image of a damaged man. "Mark's brain works just fine," she replied.

"Good enough to be a dad." It was a statement rather than a question.

April sighed, unsure how to address Brian's statement. "Brian, before a man can be a good dad, he has to want to be a dad. I don't think Mark wants to be a father.''

"Did he tell you that?''

"No, not in so many words,'' she hedged. It was the truth, Mark hadn't said he didn't want to be a father, but in saying he had no plans to become a husband, he'd implied the same about fatherhood.

"If he didn't tell you that, then you can't know for sure,'' Brian replied. "He just doesn't know how cool it would be.'' He gifted April with a reassuring smile. "I just have to show him what a cool son I'd make.''

"Honey, it's a lot more complicated than that,'' April protested.

Brian yawned, then snuggled into his pillow. "Don't worry, Mom. It'll be all right.''

April left the bedroom, her heart breaking for her son. Damn Derrick. Damn Derrick, not for leaving her, but for abandoning Brian without a backward glance. April's father had momentarily filled the void in Brian, but his unexpected death had only served to reopen the wound of abandonment.

Brian hoped to fill that void with Mark, but April knew better. Mark seemed to have too many holes in himself to be able to fill anyone else's.

So, what was he doing, coming to their cottage, sharing not only time but laughter and pleasure with them? There were times he seemed as needy, as hungry as Brian for some sort of connection.

He looked at her with want in his eyes, yet when she tried for any emotional closeness, he ran for the hills.

She undressed quickly and crawled into bed. And what was she doing? Longing for a man's touch. Not any man, but Mark's. Even knowing he was a bad bet for the future, she couldn't stop wanting him.

If she were strong, she would cut her losses where he was concerned, make sure she was unavailable when those dark gray eyes of his beckoned to her with heat.

She closed her eyes, summoning the inner strength she knew she possessed. She and Mark had made an initial mistake in making love. She had been weak and foolish to allow it to happen. She would be crazy to compound the mistake by allowing it to happen again.

By making love to him again, she knew she would tumble from the precipice where she teetered, going from falling in love with Mark to being in love with Mark.

And she couldn't allow that to happen. She didn't think she could handle being in love with the wrong man yet again.

She awoke the next morning with the strength of her conviction burning inside her like a fever. She needed to direct her relationship with Mark back into safe territory, and that meant no more games of cards, no more nights of talking beneath the moon and definitely no more making love.

She told herself she wasn't doing it just for her own sake, but for Brian's, as well. Apparently, Brian had subconsciously picked up on something between Mark and April, something that made him believe a long-term relationship was a possibility between the two adults.

But April knew it wasn't fair to Brian to invite a man into their lives who had no intention of being

permanent. Brian had already had more than his share
of inconsistent men in his life. He didn't need another
one.

It was nearly seven when she left her office and
headed back to her cottage. It had been an unusually
long day. She'd had the office to herself as Walter
hadn't been in. She'd fielded questions from guests,
arranged transportation to and from town and tried
desperately not to think about Mark.

She'd shared lunch with Brian, then had sent him
to the cottage with a list of chores and the understand-
ing that he was not to leave until she got home that
evening.

She was halfway from the main house to the cottages when Doreen stopped her. "Have you heard?"
Doreen asked, excitement vibrating her voice.

"Heard what?"

"They found Lenny Boles."

"What? Where?" April grabbed Doreen's hands.
"Did he confess to killing Marietta? To hurting
Mark?"

"He didn't confess to anything. He's dead, apparently murdered. And from what I heard, he's been
dead for a long time."

"Oh, no…" April's voice trailed off with disappointment. She'd hoped in finding Lenny, they'd have
all the answers and Mark could finally find some
peace. But if Lenny had killed Marietta, then who had
killed Lenny?

"His body was found someplace out in the desert.
The word is he's been dead since about the time Marietta was murdered."

"Where's Mark? Does he know?"

"I don't know. There's a powwow going on in the stables. I'd guess he's in there with his family and the sheriff. Both Johnna and Luke showed up a few minutes ago."

April looked toward the stables, where several officers were standing before the doors, looking officious and somber. She wondered how Mark was taking the news, exactly what Lenny Boles's death meant to Marietta's murder.

She wanted to talk to Mark, to offer comfort if he needed it. But she couldn't very well burst into a meeting behind closed doors. She'd have to wait.

"This certainly kinks up our initial speculation that Boles was responsible for Marietta's death and Mark's injuries," Sheriff Broder said, a deep frown creasing his broad forehead.

"That's certainly the understatement of the year," Johnna said dryly.

Broder ignored her. "From the initial examination of the body, I'd say Boles died about the same time as the Lopez woman."

"And that certainly sets up an interesting question. If Boles killed Marietta, then who killed Boles?" Matthew looked from one to the other, his face pale with stress.

The stress of guilt? Mark watched his brothers' and sister's faces carefully, looking for the whisper of secrets in their eyes, the hint of subterfuge.

The discovery of Lenny Boles's body had shocked Mark. Although he'd never really believed the man had been responsible for the attack, he hadn't expected Boles to turn up dead.

"We're going to have to reinterview folks around here," Sheriff Broder said. "Somebody has to know something about this."

"Is it possible to keep this investigation low-key?" Matthew asked. "I don't want our guests upset by all this."

The ranch, Mark thought. Matthew was always thinking first and foremost about the ranch. Mark turned his gaze to Johnna. She had always professed to hate the ranch. Would she involve herself in something illegal in order to cause the final demise of the place?

And then there was Luke, the wild one of the group. If he'd become involved in anything illegal, it would have been more for the thrill than for any real profit.

Suddenly Mark was sickened, sickened by the deaths that had occurred, sickened by his own tortured thoughts. "You might check Larry Greco," he said to Broder.

Jeffrey Broder's eyebrows rose in surprise. "What do you know about Greco?"

Mark shrugged. "Just that he comes around here a lot." It was all Mark was willing to offer. He grinned vacuously. "Larry and Billy are friends."

"Billy Carr?" Broder asked.

Mark nodded. "Can I go now?"

"Is there anything more we can do here?" Luke asked.

"I suppose we're through for now," Sheriff Broder replied. "I'll keep you all posted on what we discover."

The moment the sheriff dismissed them, Mark

quickly saddled up his horse. He had to get away from here...get some breathing room...some thinking room.

Once he was on the back of his horse, he exploded from the stables, giving the horse full rein, allowing the hot air to whip him in the face, whip all feeling, all thoughts out of his head.

April saw Mark leave the stable, riding as if he was attempting to outrun demons.

She turned to her friend. "Doreen, would you mind keeping an eye on Brian? I really need to talk to Mark."

"Go. Don't worry about Brian. He can spend the night with us. I'll go get him right now." She released April's hands and shooed her away.

April flashed her a grateful smile, then turned and raced for her car. She hoped he was riding for his place, hoped she could find his house on her own.

Surely now he'd realize it was time to drop his pretense and go to the sheriff with everything he knew.

Dusk was falling as she parked in front of the house. A light shone from the kitchen window, and his horse was tied out front, letting her know he was indeed there.

He answered the door at her first knock. "April, what are you doing here?" He pulled her inside and closed the door.

She saw the tension that drew his features taut, the shadows of darkness that clung in the depths of his eyes. "I wanted to make sure you were all right."

"I'm all right." He led her to the sofa. After she

sat, he sank down heavily next to her, as if the weight
on his shoulders was too massive to handle. He raked
a hand through his hair and looked at her. "Two dead
people and no suspects. No, I guess I'm not okay after
all."

She leaned toward him and placed a hand on his
forearm, feeling the tension that gripped his body.
"Mark, I'm afraid for you. Go to the sheriff, tell him
what you know. Go to your family, tell them the
truth."

"The discovery of Boles's body doesn't change
anything as far as I'm concerned," he countered. He
raked a hand through his hair once again. "I still
don't know who to trust."

"But you have to trust somebody," she exclaimed,
and tightened her grip on his arm. At that moment
she recognized it was too late for her to hold back
from loving him. She already did.

He shook his head. "Sooner or later I'm going to
figure out what's going on, what had Marietta so
frightened and ultimately what got her killed. I've got
to do this my way."

"Why?" She pulled her hand back from him, anger coursing through her. "Why does it have to be
your way? Why do you have to do this all alone?"

He stood up, his eyes suddenly blazing with an
anger of his own. "Because that's the way it's always
been, that's the way I've always been—alone."

He paced back and forth in front of her, energy
wafting from him. "I've never been able to depend
on anyone but myself. Something is wrong here at the
ranch, and I've got to figure out what it is." His hands
clenched at his sides. "I need to fix things."

A sudden realization came to April's mind. "Why, Mark? Why does it have to be you alone that fixes things?" She got up and approached him, halting when she stood mere inches from him.

"It just has to be this way." His eyes were dark pools of pain, and April saw not only the man, but the tormented little boy who desperately needed his father's approval.

"Mark, your father is dead. You can't be the hero that saves the ranch for him."

For a brief moment she thought she'd gone too far, spoken too freely. He seemed to rise in height, expand in breadth, and a flash of rage sparked in his eyes.

He glared at her as if she were personally responsible for everything—for his father's indifference, for Mark's dysfunctional relationship with his siblings, for his suspicion of them, for the very core of loneliness she'd sensed in him.

She gasped as he grabbed her by the upper arms and pulled her toward him. "Don't you understand?" His voice was less anger and more anguish. "I have to do this for me. I have to know that I can do something worthwhile, that I'm important."

April's heart wept for him. Although her father and Derrick had taken much from her, she'd never lost her sense of self-worth. She placed the palms of her hands on the sides of his face. "Mark, I believe you're important and worthwhile. I believe in you."

Her words seemed to transform whatever anguish, whatever anger he'd been feeling, into something very different. His eyes once again blazed, but this time with a need that stole her breath away.

He crashed his lips down to hers in a kiss that

shouted of hunger and need. At the same time his
arms surrounded her and pulled her so close she felt
that he was attempting to pull her into him.

Someplace in the back of April's mind she knew
what was about to happen, but her earlier conviction
seemed unimportant as Mark's kiss devoured all other
thought but his need for her and hers for him.

Chapter 11

While their initial lovemaking had been slow and easy—the tentative exploring of new lovers—there was nothing slow or easy about it this time.

Mark's kiss consumed her with fiery need as his hands stroked down the length of her back. When he reached the small of her back, he pressed her harder against him, letting her know the full extent of his arousal.

His mouth left hers, trailing hot kisses down the side of her neck. His hands moved up beneath her T-shirt, caressing the bare skin of her back, but the caressing lasted only a moment before he pulled the shirt over her head.

Even if she'd wanted to protest, had wanted to halt him, he gave her no opportunity, sweeping her into a maelstrom of passion that made thought of anything but him impossible.

She didn't know if he removed her clothes or she did. She only knew that moments later they were both naked and on the floor of the living room.

There was little foreplay, their desire for each other too great to spend time caressing or stroking. She already felt as if they'd indulged in hours, days of foreplay. She was ready for him, had been ready since the moment of his initial kiss.

His hands moved to the sides of her face as he kissed her with a depth that consumed her. At the same time he entered her, filling her with pulsating heat.

Frantic, with a touch of desperation, they moved together. April was unsure what forces drove Mark, but she knew the force that drove her—love.

She had no idea when exactly she'd fallen in love with Mark. Perhaps it had been that morning when she'd seen him with Brian, polishing saddles in the stable, when he'd shown eternal patience and kindness to a child who desperately needed those qualities.

Or maybe her love for him had blossomed amid the magic of their first kiss beneath a big coyote moon. It really didn't matter when she'd fallen in love with him. What mattered was the depth and breadth of her love for him.

It filled her, permeating every fiber of her being. She loved him as she'd never loved Derrick, as she'd never loved before.

"April...April." He whispered her name over and over again as he moved against her, into her very soul. She clutched at his back, kissed the hollow of his throat as they moved faster, seeking the rhythm that would ultimately release them.

Frenzied, almost savagely they met each other, as if consumed by a single need. He whispered in her ear, soft whispers of passion as he drove deep.

The release came to her first, and tears sprang to her eyes as wave after wave of pleasure crashed through her. He followed just behind her, stiffening against her and crying out hoarsely.

For a long moment neither of them spoke. Mark moved slightly to the side so his entire weight wasn't resting on her. April was aware of her heartbeat slowing, seeking a more normal rhythm.

Mark leaned up on his elbow and gazed down at her. "You all right?"

She nodded, too full of emotion to speak.

"I'm sorry." He touched her cheek with his fingertip, a gesture so tender, so sweet, she felt tears once again burning at her eyes. "I didn't mean for this to happen. Especially not so—so fiercely."

She smiled dryly. "As I recall, I wasn't exactly an unwilling participant in the fierceness."

Her love for him filled her, begging to be released, but she held it in, knowing it was the last thing Mark would want to hear. Instead of speaking of her love, she loved him with her eyes, taking in each and every feature of his face and memorizing it in her heart.

"If you don't stop looking at me like that, we're going to have a problem," he said, his voice a deep growl.

She laughed, loving the fact that she could affect him by merely looking at him. "Surely it would be a problem we could solve."

"You are a wicked woman," he teased. In one smooth, graceful movement, he rolled off her and stood. He held out a hand to help her up off the floor. "Have you eaten supper?"

"No, I was on my way to the cottage from the house when I heard the news about Lenny."

"Where's Brian?"

It warmed her heart that he would even think about her son. "With Doreen for the night."

"How about a fast shower, then I'll fix us some omelettes?" He didn't give her an opportunity to accept or decline. Taking her by the hand, he led her through his bedroom and into the master bath.

She stood and watched while he adjusted the water temperature in the large shower, surprised to discover it seemed perfectly natural to be naked with Mark.

And in his nakedness he was impressive. Dark hair curled on his chest, covering the center, then tapering to a thin line that ran the length of his flat abdomen. He looked powerful, utterly male, and gazing at him made breathing a little more difficult.

When he had the water to his liking and steam began to fill the glass enclosure, he stepped into the shower and pulled her in with him.

April wasn't sure what was more sensually appealing, the waterfall of the warm water caressing her skin or Mark's body moving intimately against hers. In her three years of marriage, she'd never showered with Derrick. She'd never showered with any man in her life.

She watched as he took a bar of soap and lathered a spongeful of suds, then he rubbed the sponge down her neck and across her breasts.

A moment before, April had believed herself completely sated, as fulfilled and satisfied as a woman could be. However, she felt herself responding anew to his touch.

When he finished washing her breasts, he pulled her against him so he could reach behind and stroke the sponge down the length of her back.

She hissed at the exquisite pleasure that soared through her. As he touched her more intimately, her knees weakened and she sagged against him.

Every sense she possessed was heightened as she'd never experienced before. The scent of the minty soap whirled in her head as she took the sponge from him and began to lather his chest.

Before long, both their bodies were soft and slick with soap and water. They moved together and the tactile pleasure of skin against skin, mouth against mouth, beneath the warmth of the water fed the fuel of April's desire higher.

Apparently the experience affected Mark in the same way. With his eyes blazing an inferno of renewed want, he took the soap from her, pulled her beneath the full shower spray to rinse off, then shut off the water and carried her from the shower to the bed.

There they made love slowly, languidly. Gone was the utter desperation that had earlier marked their lovemaking. In its place was a simple quiet need for each other, a need that was all encompassing.

Afterward they once again lay quiet in each other's arms, the sheets beneath them a tangle of material. The room had grown dark with night, and only the light from the bathroom illuminated the bedroom.

"I told you it was a problem we could solve," she said softly.

He laughed, the laughter vibrating in her chest as she remained firmly against him. She could feel his heartbeat pounding against her own, and the sound of those mingling beats sent a symphony of love singing inside her.

She longed to tell Mark that she loved him. Her need to confess her innermost feelings for him burned inside her. But she kept her silence.

Although he appeared to be relaxed next to her, his eyes closed and his breathing regular, she sensed a tension still rolling around inside him.

Besides, he hadn't uttered any words of love. He'd cried her name, whispered sweet and sexy things in her ear, but he hadn't spoken of love.

Or had he? Hadn't she tasted love in his kisses, felt love flowing from his fingertips as he'd stroked her so tenderly? Had that been love? Or the finesse of a man adept at soothing both animals and women?

He'd told her he had no plans to marry, had implied he would never have a family, and yet never had she met a man more qualified to be both. Never, before Mark, had she met a man who seemed to ache with the need for both.

"Hungry?" His deep voice finally broke the silence between them.

"Not really." She turned her head to look at him, loving the strength of his features. She knew that strength had been carved out not only from the barren land in which he lived, but also from his harsh childhood devoid of love.

"Tomorrow morning we're having a family meeting." He frowned, as if the thought was an unpleasant one. "One of the stipulations in Dad's will is that once a week we have a family meeting with Walter."

April didn't say anything, although she wondered why he was telling her this. He rolled over on his back and threw an arm across his eyes. "After the meeting, I'll go into town and talk to the sheriff."

"And you'll tell your family?"

He sighed. "No, not yet. But I will tell the sheriff everything I know."

April laid her head on his chest. "Thank you," she said softly. Relief flooded through her. Although she believed he should talk to his family first, it wasn't her call. It was enough that he intended to tell the sheriff, and perhaps Broder could figure out why Marietta had been killed and what exactly was going on at the ranch.

She remained with her head on his chest for a little while, listening to his heart throbbing in a slow rhythm. After several minutes his hand stroked through her hair, a soothing, sweet touch that summoned the first edge of sleepiness.

Reluctantly she sat up. "I should go."

He touched her arm and she turned to gaze at him. "Why? Brian is at Doreen's for the night. There's no reason you have to go." His hand moved up her arm and he touched the side of her cheek with his index finger. "Stay with me, April. Stay the night, and I'll see that you're back at the cottage early."

April knew she shouldn't, knew that to sleep in his arms would only deepen the love she felt for him. Sleeping with him seemed every bit as intimate as

making love to him. And yet, how could she deny
herself this?

Somehow she felt in her heart that things were
coming to a climax between herself and Mark, that
when he told the sheriff the truth in the morning,
Mark would no longer need her.

As the only person who had known the truth about
him, she'd been an outlet for him, a person with
whom he could let down his guard and speak freely.

Although she had fallen in love with him, she had
no idea what his true feelings for her were. They appeared to be as hidden as his intelligence was beneath
his facade.

"April, stay the night, sleep in my arms."

She knew the right thing was to get up and leave,
but she was helpless against the force of his gaze,
beneath the touch of his hand. She allowed him to
pull her into his arms and against the warmth of his
body.

As they settled in together, he pulled a sheet over
them, as if protecting them from the night and any
outside forces that might threaten.

With a contentment she'd never known, she closed
her eyes and fell asleep as love for Mark filled her
heart.

Mark found sleep elusive. Despite the fact that
April's body was warm against his, that her closeness
filled him with a euphoric rightness, his mind refused
to shut off enough to allow sleep to overtake him.

The discovery of Lenny's body had been shocking,
and he felt as if it had somehow forced his hand. How
much longer could he play the fool without results?

If he were to guess what had happened, he'd speculate that Lenny, who'd had a crush on Marietta, had followed the woman on that fatal night. He'd seen whoever had killed her, the person who had attempted to kill Mark, and he'd died because he'd been in the wrong place at the wrong time.

He shifted positions, careful not to disturb April's sleep. The old barn. He believed the answers began and ended in the old barn. Marietta had doodled *barn* endlessly in her notes.

But what did it mean? What were the answers? He frowned as something niggled at the back of his brain, some little piece of information that begged to be acknowledged. No matter how hard he tried to identify it, it wouldn't come.

He tightened his arms around April. She wanted him to tell his family the truth, but he was reluctant to do so, and adamant that she not learn the reason for his reluctance.

His frown deepened as he played and replayed the conversation he'd heard between Billy Carr and Larry Greco. Billy had mentioned "the boss." Mark wanted to know what was going on but, more important, he needed to know who was responsible. Who was "the boss"?

And in the depths of his heart his fear was that it might be one of his brothers or his sister. How long could he carry this burden, this fear, that brought deep shame and a tremendous sense of disloyalty that weighed heavy on his heart.

April moaned faintly in her sleep, as if protesting his thoughts. He stroked her back, and she instantly calmed. April. Her very name caused a rivulet of warmth to flow through him.

He realized that his mind had been assessing and reassessing the possible crimes and criminals on the ranch because it was easier, less complicated than dealing with his emotions where April was concerned.

She filled a void he hadn't realized he'd had. Her smile warmed his heart and evoked laughter inside him. The pain of her past had somehow become his pain.

He loved her.

The joy this realization brought with it was short-lived. He loved her, and if he had his way he would continue their relationship as it was at this moment. Stealing nights when possible to hold her in his arms, spending evenings with her and Brian, sharing in the love that existed between mother and son.

If he had his way they would continue with their relationship of no commitment, no expectations, no real future. Because it was easier that way.

He could successfully fulfill no expectations, and she'd never have to know he was a failure, as his father had known, as Rachel had discovered.

He loved April with every fiber of his being, and that was why he would never promise her a future, never make any sort of commitment to her.

She and Brian deserved a man who was better, a man who could provide a loving, supportive, extended family. They both deserved better than a man who was good for nothing but working with livestock.

Again he tightened his arms around her, reveling in the scent of her, the feel of her body warm and compliant against his own.

Closing his eyes, he felt his mind finally emptying of all thought other than this moment of holding April while she slept. They may not have a future together, but he had until dawn to hold her. And for the moment that was enough.

He awakened before dawn, instantly aware of what had been niggling at his mind concerning the old barn. He fought the impulse to awaken April and share with her what was on his mind.

Darkness still claimed the sky and April slept soundly in his arms. No point in awakening her yet. He checked his wristwatch, the luminous dial letting him know it was just after four. Dawn was only an hour away. He could wait.

Besides, waking with a beautiful naked woman in his arms was a novelty. In all his thirty-three years, he'd never actually slept the entire night with a woman.

When he and Rachel had been dating, she'd lived in an apartment building in town and hadn't wanted him leaving her house in the mornings in case the neighbors might see. But now, looking back, he realized she hadn't wanted the ultimate intimacy of sleeping in his arms.

Since Rachel, there had been no woman Mark had wanted to hold through the night, awaken to in the morning. Not until April.

He gazed at her now, taking pleasure in studying her features in leisure. In sleep she looked younger. He knew she must be about around thirty years old, but sleep erased ten years from her face.

She was beautiful, and her beauty ached inside him

because he wanted her for a lifetime, but knew he couldn't, shouldn't, have her.

Mark had spent his youth as the invisible middle son. He'd spent much of his adulthood as the invisible man. Being with April transformed him, made him feel visible for the first time in his life, but he didn't trust the transformation. He knew that eventually he'd go back to being nothing, nobody, and April deserved better, just as Rachel had.

Dawn light was streaking across the sky when April opened her eyes and smiled. "Good morning," she said. "How long have you been awake?"

"About an hour or so."

Neither of them moved from the warmth of their entanglement beneath the covers. "And what have you been doing for the past hour?"

"Thinking."

She gazed at him intently. "You haven't changed your mind, have you? About going to the sheriff?"

He rubbed a hand down her back, loving the feel of her skin against his fingers. "No, I haven't changed my mind."

"Good," she said firmly.

"But—"

"I hate 'buts,'" she said, interrupting him. She untangled herself from him and sat up, holding the sheet over her breasts with a sense of modesty.

He sat up, as well. "I've been thinking about the old barn," he began.

"What about it?" She frowned.

"I still think something isn't right there."

April's brow wrinkled in perplexity. "But we

checked it out. We didn't find anything suspicious, nothing odd at all.''

"Ever since we went there something has been bothering me about the place.'' Mark raked a hand through his sleep-tousled hair, the realization about the barn that had been so illuminating an hour ago now seeming far reaching. "I don't know, maybe it's nothing.''

April placed a hand on his forearm. "Tell me,'' she urged.

"When we were out at the barn and we were looking around inside, there were no footsteps in the dirt and dust on the floor.''

She stared at him in bewilderment. "I don't understand... That just means nobody had been out there before us.''

"But there should have been animal prints. Lizards and rodents, jackrabbits and who knows what else, would find the barn a perfect place to roam.''

"We saw a lizard, remember? It scared us when it raced across the floor.''

He nodded. "And when it ran across the floor, it left behind little footprints. I can't believe that was the first animal to run across that floor, and I keep seeing that broom standing in the corner.''

Again April's forehead creased with thought. "You think maybe somebody swept the floor to make it appear nobody had been there?''

He shrugged. "Isn't it possible?''

"Sure,'' she agreed.

"So, it's not a crazy thought?''

She laughed, her gaze on him soft. "Mark, you're

about the most *un*crazy person I've ever known. So, what are you going to do?''

''Check it out one more time.''

''I'll come with you.'' He looked at her in surprise, and she smiled. ''Two people looking at something might find what one person misses.'' She swung her feet over the side of the bed. ''Besides, the barn won't scare me at dawn like it might scare me at dusk.''

''There's no guarantee that bogeymen come out only at night,'' Mark observed.

She slid off the bed and walked to the bathroom door. ''But I'm not afraid of bogeymen if I'm with you.'' With that statement of utter trust, she disappeared into the bathroom.

Mark rolled over on his back and stared up at the ceiling that was painted with the colors of dawn. Once again his thoughts were in turmoil where April was concerned.

Somehow he'd garnered her complete and utter trust, and that scared him. With trust came responsibility, and the last thing Mark wanted was to be responsible for anyone.

He rolled out of bed and grabbed his clothes, then went into the hall bathroom for a quick shower.

By the time he was finished showering and dressing, April was waiting for him.

He felt the need to say something to her, to warn her not to rely on him, not to trust him. He wanted to tell her not to love him and to have no expectations of him despite what they had shared the night before.

However, he wasn't sure how to broach it. After all, she had spoken no words of love to him. In fact, she had told him after they'd made love the first time that the last thing she wanted was another man in her life. She'd indicated that sex with him was enough for her.

"Should I just follow you to the barn?" she asked as they left the house.

"No, I'll ride with you in the car," he replied.

She gestured to the big mare tethered to the hitching post in front of the house. "What about your horse?"

He untied the reins and slapped the horse on the rump. "Home," he said, and the horse took off running. "She'll go back to the stables."

Together they got into April's car, Mark behind the wheel. As always the sunrise was splendid as vivid colors splashed across the sky in the promise of a new day.

"You still don't intend to tell your brothers and sister the truth?" she asked once they were underway.

"No, I'm not willing to give up my act yet. It's the only thing that has given me any kind of information at all. At least I know for sure that whatever is going on, Billy Carr and Larry Greco are in it up to their teeth."

"And you'll tell the sheriff that?"

He nodded. "Absolutely. And there's another reason why I'm not willing to give up my act yet." He looked over at her and noticed how dawn's light painted her features in a soft glow. Her face was scrubbed clean, without a stitch of makeup, and yet she still radiated a beauty that affected him on a profound level.

"What's that?" she asked.

He frowned and once again focused his attention

out the front window. "Whoever hit me over the head at this moment believes that I'm too damaged to remember anything Marietta might have told me that night. If I confess that I'm unharmed mentally, then I become a threat once again."

April gasped. "I hadn't thought about that."

"The thought of becoming a target doesn't scare me," he continued. "But right now I believe I have the edge. If I tell everyone the truth, then I feel like I'll lose that edge."

He parked the car outside the barn, then turned to her. "Let's get this over with so I can put my mind to rest concerning this place."

Together they got out of the car and approached the barn. The double door was halfway open, allowing the morning light to slash into the darkness. Mark pulled it all the way open, further illuminating the interior, then he and April stepped inside.

Instantly Mark's adrenaline pumped as he saw the utter smoothness of the floor in front of them. "This isn't right," he said, more to himself than to her. "There should be marks on the floor." He turned to look at April. "There's not even one sign of our footsteps from when we were here before."

He walked over to the corner and grabbed the broom. Methodically he began to sweep the dust to expose the wooden floorboards beneath.

"What are you looking for?" April asked, then coughed as dust swirled in the air.

"I'm not sure," he replied. And he wasn't. He only knew that it appeared that somebody had gone to great lengths to make certain the dust evenly covered the floor.

April moved behind him as the gritty dust and sand continued to fly, exposing more and more of the flooring beneath.

Adrenaline pumped through him as he bared the edge of a trap door in the floor. "April, look." Hurriedly he swept to expose the rest of the door. When he was finished, April gripped his arm painfully tight.

"What do you think is down there?" she asked, her voice a cautious whisper.

"Maybe nothing, or maybe evidence that will tell us exactly what's been going on." Mark bent down to grab the metal ring that would open the door.

"Well, well, if it isn't the half-wit and his honey."

Mark straightened and whirled around to see Billy Carr behind them, a grin on his face and a gun pointed directly at them.

Chapter 12

"For a man who doesn't have all his cornflakes in one box, you've become a real pain in the ass," Billy said.

"What's going on here, Billy?" Mark asked. At the same time he placed his body between Billy and April.

April's heart felt as if it might explode from her chest. Although Billy's face held a smile, it was not a pleasant gesture, rather it was a grin that reflected the mean spirit, the evil heart of the man who brandished it.

"How come you've got a gun, Billy?" Mark asked, and in the slight singsong rhythm of his words, April realized he was attempting to play his fool role once again.

Billy's eyes narrowed, and the smirk on his lips fell aside. "Don't play with me, Mark. I heard enough to know you aren't as half-witted as you've been pretending.''

''So, what are you going to do? Shoot me for being smarter than you thought?''

April gripped Mark's arm, wanting to stop him from baiting Billy, afraid of what Billy might do if Mark pushed him too far.

''I'll shoot you if I have to,'' Billy returned. ''But it will probably be up to the boss what happens to the two of you. If I was to guess, you'll end up someplace out in the desert as food for the buzzards just like Lenny did.''

April tightened her grip on Mark's arm, fighting panic.

''And who is this boss?'' Mark asked.

Billy grinned. ''You'll just have to wait and see.''

''So, it was you who killed Marietta? Who tried to kill me?'' Mark's body was a single strand of taut energy.

''Nah, that was the boss man himself. Marietta just couldn't leave things alone and she had to drag you into the whole thing. Then that damned Lenny saw what happened to the two of you and he had to be taken care of. We had to protect ourselves. Larry,'' he bellowed suddenly. ''Git down here. I need your help.''

Mark and April looked up as Larry Greco descended the stairs from the loft. Now there were two men with guns facing them.

As if sensing April's incredible fear, Mark grabbed her hand and squeezed tightly.

''What are we gonna do now?'' Larry asked, his eyes wild with anxiety as he looked at Mark and

April. "This whole thing has gotten out of control, way out of control. I told you I wanted out."

"Shut up," Billy snapped. "We're going to make certain these two can't do anything to screw up the operation." He gestured toward the door in the floor. "Open it up."

Despite April's enormous fear and the knowledge that she and Mark were in danger, curiosity filled her as Larry moved to the door.

"It's got to be drugs," Mark said more to himself than to anyone else. "They've got to be running drugs from here."

Billy snorted and grinned. "Just shows you aren't as smart as you think you are. Selling drugs is for fools."

"Then what? What in the hell is going on?" Mark's voice was deep and gruff with anger.

Larry opened the door, then stepped back, his gun still trained on Mark and April.

"Come on out, everyone," Billy yelled.

April gasped as men began crawling up out of the hole in the floor. There were five in all, five Mexican men who chattered to each other in Spanish as they bent and stretched to alleviate cramped muscles.

"Illegal aliens," Mark said flatly.

"Ah, but not just any illegal aliens," Billy replied. "These are members of the Juarez family, extremely wealthy men and head of one of the largest drug cartels in Mexico. Unfortunately, the Mexican army has been making life and work miserable for them lately, so they've decided to relocate to the States."

"But the United States wouldn't exactly welcome

them in with open arms.'' Again Mark's voice was flat and emotionless.

"That's right," Billy replied. "They're all convicted felons, but they're very generous with those who help them. We hold them here while Larry works up some impeccable identification.''

"And you've done this for others, as well?" Mark's disgust was obvious.

"This is our fourth group," Billy boasted. "Now get in the hole.''

April's heart clenched in her chest, making breathing difficult as she eyed the dark hole in the ground. It looked like a grave. She feared it would be her grave.

Mark's hand once again tightened around hers, as if he'd read her thoughts and was attempting to give her courage.

"Come on, let's go," Billy said impatiently.

April cast a frantic look at the five men who stood nearby, watching the unfolding scene with interest. However, there was no compassion, no commiseration on any of their faces, nothing to indicate they might be inclined to help her or Mark. Convicted felons, drug lords, they weren't going to help them.

Together Mark and April moved to the door. She peered down, seeing that against one wall was a wooden ladder that lead down into the dark depths.

"Billy, let April go," Mark said. "She won't tell anyone what she's seen here.''

Again Billy snorted a burst of unpleasant laughter. "Yeah, right, now you're talking like you think *I* have brain damage. Come on, I'm losing patience here. Get down there so I can go get the boss and tell him what's happening."

With trembling arms and legs, April lowered herself onto the ladder and descended into the darkness below. To her surprise, there were only seven long stairs before her feet touched the bottom.

She stood on the earthen floor and looked up, expecting to see Mark descending just behind her. Suddenly there were sounds of a scuffle, a grunt of pain, then Mark fell through the hole and landed, half sitting at her feet.

"Mark!" She crouched next to him. "Are you all right?" she asked, her fingertips fluttering over his face, across his shoulders.

"Yeah, although I think I have a new lump on my head." He shifted positions and pulled her to sit next to him, their backs against the enclosure wall. "I tried to get to my gun, but Billy realized what I was doing. He grabbed it first and cracked me over the head."

At that moment the door overhead slammed shut, casting them into the most profound darkness April had ever known. Her heart raced a frantic rhythm as fear gripped her in icy fingers.

Mark put an arm around her shoulder and she leaned into him, resting her head against the front of his shirt. Slowly the panic ebbed, although her heart continued to beat far too fast.

"April, I'm sorry." His arm tightened around her. "I'm so sorry I got you into this." His voice was low, deep with torment.

She reached up and placed a hand on the side of his face. "Shh. You didn't get me into anything. I came with you this morning of my own will." She laughed, and in that laughter heard a touch of her own hysteria. ''Who'd have thought that the bogeymen would be up and working at dawn?''

He tightened his embrace of her and for a few long minutes they remained silent, simply holding on to each other. Sounds drifted down from the barn above, the creaking of floorboards as somebody walked across them, a low murmur of voices broken by an occasional burst of laughter.

What was going to happen to them? How long would they be in this hole in the ground?

Brian.

What was going to happen to Brian? April tried not to think of her son, knowing that thoughts of Brian would drive her insane. She tried not to think of how desperate their situation seemed to be, knowing that, too, would make her crazy.

She had to maintain control, had to sustain hope that somehow they'd get out of this mess. ''Will somebody come looking for you?'' she asked.

''I don't know… Probably not until I don't show up for the family meeting. That's at nine. What about you? Will Brian tell somebody you aren't at home?''

''Eventually.'' She frowned. ''But he doesn't work at the stables this morning, so who knows what time he and Ricky will get up and around. It could be noon before he realizes I'm missing.'' Her voice cracked with emotion as she thought of her son, alone and frightened, wondering what had happened to her.

Mark cursed, a muttering of violent frustration. He sighed and stroked her hair with his hand. In his touch, she felt his regret, his anger that she'd become embroiled in this whole mess.

She was angry, too. For both of them. Angry that men would go to any lengths for money, angry that the Delaney Dude Ranch, a place that should have been for good, clean fun and relaxation, had become the location for criminal activity.

"At least now you know," she said. "Now you know what Marietta had wanted to tell you. Exactly what's been going on out here."

"Yeah, but knowing *what* isn't enough. I want to know who."

"Do you have any idea who the boss might be?" she asked. She could feel his heartbeat beneath her cheek, and at her question it stepped up its rhythm.

"No," he replied, but there was a lack of conviction in his answer. "I can't tell you for sure who the boss is, but I can tell you what I fear." He hesitated for a long moment. "I'm afraid that it's Luke or Matthew or Johnna." The words flew out of him as if beneath an enormous pressure.

April stirred against him. "Oh, Mark, surely you can't really believe that. Although I don't know your brothers and sister well, surely you can't think any of them have anything to do with all this."

"I don't know them well enough to know what they're capable of." Again his voice was deep and filled with the torment of his thoughts. "I have agonized over this. I don't want to believe any of them capable...but I just don't know."

"But, Mark, you grew up with them. How could you not know them well enough to know what they are capable of?" April struggled to understand the dynamics between the Delaney children. "Surely you must know in your heart that your own family wouldn't murder Marietta, wouldn't try to kill you.''

''Did you know your own father well enough to realize he was capable of stealing all your money?''

April frowned thoughtfully. She leaned away from him and instead placed her back against the wall. Although their shoulders still touched, she needed a bit of distance to think properly.

''You know, it's funny. For all this time since my father's death, I've felt betrayed, like he'd intentionally cheated me, and I couldn't understand how he would do such a thing, not just to me, but to Brian.''

She was surprised to realize her sense of betrayal was gone, and without it the truth of the situation was evident. ''But I know now that isn't true.''

''What do you mean?''

April wished there was some light, so she could look into Mark's eyes. She'd feel better, more at ease, if she could see him. ''My father loved me. He would never have intentionally hurt me. He was weak and foolish, and probably believed he'd be able to make me money by spending my money. But I know he didn't intentionally mean to cheat me. People who truly love you don't deliberately hurt you.''

''That may be your experience, but it hasn't been mine.'' There was a touch of bitterness in his voice.

''Tell me, Mark. Tell me about growing up with your family.'' April touched his arm to encourage him.

Vaguely, in the back of her mind, she knew what she was doing—trying to keep her mind off the fact that they were in an earthen tomb, waiting for death to come to them.

* * *

Mark raked a hand down his face, frustration, regret and rage creating a tumble of emotions inside him. He was frustrated with his helplessness, regretting the fact that April was now at risk because of his need to be a lone ranger. Finally, he was raging inside at the knowledge that somebody had used his home to bring criminal, illegal aliens into the country.

He mentally attempted to shove through the emotion and delve back into his past, a past he'd tried for years not to think about.

He shifted positions and stretched his legs out before him in an attempt to avoid getting cramped. "We were raised not to trust each other, to compete against one another for my father's attention, his approval and ultimately his love."

Mark shook his head as memory after memory assailed him, and along with the memories came an ache in his chest. "My father was such a difficult man, so hard, so cold, and we kids were all so needy, so eager to please him."

He couldn't explain everything to her. The heartless words his father would spout, the fists that flew due to some imagined slight and the subtle manipulation that pitted child against child. Some of it was simply too painful to revisit.

"Most of the time Matthew was my father's obvious favorite, and he guarded that position very carefully, tattling on the rest of us whenever we did something wrong." Subconsciously Mark rubbed the lump that had risen on the back of his head where Billy had clunked him with the gun butt, welcoming the edge of pain that accompanied his touch.

"Johnna was usually the one in the doghouse. For some reason she garnered my father's anger faster and more often than the rest of us. Luke was the only one who could make Dad laugh. He got out of a lot of beatings by playing the fool."

"But, Mark, what would they have to gain by being the boss of an illegal alien operation?"

"Money. I'm sure those men out there are paying hundreds of thousands of dollars to get into the country with proper paperwork."

"But why would any of your family need money? None of you seem to be exactly starving." Once again she placed a hand on his arm, and her touch was more welcome than he was willing to acknowledge even to himself.

"We're all financially comfortable as long as the ranch continues to run. But if the ranch is sold and the proceeds go to our aunt Clara, then we each end up virtually penniless." Again he reached up and touched the lump on his scalp, the pain of that touch far more welcome than the pain of his thoughts.

"Maybe Matthew believes the more money he has, the better he'll be able to control the terms of the will and convince the rest of us to adhere to it. He'll do anything for the ranch."

"And what about Johnna?" April's question intruded into his thoughts. "I can't imagine that she'd have anything to do with this."

Mark sighed as he thought of his sister. "Johnna's changed a lot since she lost her baby."

"Lost her baby? What happened?"

"When she was just a little over six months pregnant, she miscarried. It's been almost eight years, but

I don't think Johnna really got over it. She got hard after that and she hates the ranch more than anything. Her law practice is nearly nonexistent, and sometimes I think she'd do anything to destroy this ranch and every memory of our father.''

He shifted positions, once again pulling April against him, wanting, needing her warmth. ''Luke would love to be independently wealthy so he could do nothing but play his guitar and romance half the town.''

April was silent for a long moment. He wished he could see her face, wondered if she found his suspicions of his siblings as abhorrent as he did. ''You told me how everyone else fit in with your father. What about you? What was your role with him?'' she asked softly.

''I was the invisible child. I tried not to gain his attention either in a negative or positive way.'' Mark leaned forward, once again scraping a hand across his lower jaw.

He wondered if he'd ever get the smell of this place out of his nose. It was not only the smell of dank clay and sand, but there were also faint odors of sweat and urine, of fear and blood.

He stood, surprising April with the abruptness of his movement. ''What are you doing?'' she asked.

''Exploring,'' he said as he used his hands to feel up and down the walls. ''Trying to discover if there's another way out of here.'' He didn't want this place to be April's grave.

He heard her as she got to her feet. For a few moments the only sound was the brush of their hands against the walls and their breathing, shallow and rapid as fear continued to grow.

When they'd felt and touched every space and realized there was no exit except the trap door, Mark pulled April into his arms and burrowed his face into the curly softness of her hair.

"I'm sorry," he murmured, his chest tight with regret. "I'm so sorry I got you into this mess."

"Shh." She pressed two fingers against his lips, then removed her fingers and rose up so her mouth was touching his.

They kissed hungrily, desperately, as if aware of time running out. Her body pressed against his, a perfect fit.

The utter hopelessness Mark felt about their situation made him realize they would never have a future together. He would never have the opportunity to let her down, to be too little. He kissed her again and knew she was silently crying, for he tasted the salt of her tears. He used his thumbs to wipe her tears, then kissed her yet again.

"We'll get out of this mess," she said as they once again sat side by side. "Somehow, someway. You wait and see, we'll get through this." She squeezed his hand.

Mark said nothing. He knew the truth. The boss who had killed Marietta, had tried to kill him and had murdered Lenny wasn't about to let them walk away from here. They were doomed.

Chapter 13

It was easy for April to lose track of time with only the beat of Mark's heart to signal its passing. In another place, at another time, her heart would be singing with joy because Mark was holding her close. But it was difficult to sustain joy while awaiting whatever fate was in store for them.

April closed her eyes, imagining how things would be if—no, *when* they got out of here and the danger was gone. She just knew in her heart that her relationship with Mark would deepen and grow. And maybe, just maybe, he would love her just a little.

She snuggled closer to Mark's side, comforted by his arm around her. "Tell me something. Talk to me," she said, wanting his deep, strong voice to momentarily carry her away from the fear that coiled deep inside her.

"What do you want me to talk about?"

"Anything," she replied. "Tell me how much you like kissing me."

She sensed the smile on his lips. "I like kissing you as much as I like anything else I can think of."

"Even better than your horse? I heard that a cowboy's horse was the most important thing in his life."

"I love my horse," Mark agreed. "But she doesn't kiss very well."

April laughed, the edge of fear apparent in her laughter.

Her laughter stopped, and she felt him tense as noise resounded above them. Heavy footsteps...deep voices... It was obvious something was happening above.

April tensed, as well, her body aching with the need to jump up and run, escape from whatever was about to occur. She gasped as the door above them opened, spilling down light that momentarily blinded her.

"Come on, both of you get up here," Billy said.

Mark turned to her, his features more taut than she'd ever seen. He touched her cheek, and she felt his love, his regret in that touch. She also saw the fear that haunted him.

She knew it wasn't the fear of death, rather it was the agony of anticipating that when they climbed out of the hole, he would possibly come face-to-face with one of his siblings.

She wrapped her arms around his waist and held him tight for a long moment.

"Come on, let's go. We don't have all day," Billy snarled.

April released Mark and with trembling arms and

legs, made her way up and out of the hole. Mark
followed just behind her and they stood before Billy,
who once again had his gun trained on them.

There was no sign of the five men who'd been
hidden in the hole, and no sign of Larry, although the
murmur of voices and the sound of footsteps drifted
down from the loft. "The boss is on his way," Billy
said.

"You'll never get away with this," Mark said. His
hands clenched at his sides. "Don't you think somebody will get suspicious if April and I are found
dead?"

Billy shrugged and gave them an easy grin. "It's
not my problem. But if I'm to guess, it's gonna be a
long time before your bodies are found."

"Then people will look for us," April said, fear
clutching at her throat and stinging at her eyes.

"I don't think so," Billy countered. "Everyone
knows you've got the hots for half-wit there. It should
be relatively easy to start a rumor that you two took
off for Mexico. Your car will be missing, along with
a suitcase full of clothes."

"Nobody will believe that I went off with Mark
and left my son," April exclaimed fervently.

Before Billy could reply, a voice called out, "Then
perhaps we can arrange for your son to join you and
Mark in your graves."

April gasped at the familiar voice and turned to see
Walter Tilley enter the barn.

"Walter," Mark exclaimed in surprise. "What in
the hell are you doing, Tilley?"

"Making my fortune." As usual, Walter was clad
in a spotless linen suit. His gray hair was meticulously

styled and he looked fresh and unruffled by the events unfolding.

"Your father was a stingy, selfish man," he said to Mark. "He didn't pay me half of my worth and I had to be resourceful in order to keep myself in the manner in which I want to be accustomed."

"And that resourcefulness includes murder?" Again Mark's hands balled into fists, and April knew he was thinking of Marietta.

Walter waved his hands as if to dismiss Mark's anger. "An unfortunate situation. Marietta wanted to use the barn for some social activity and made several trips out here. Unfortunately, on one of those trips she saw us transporting some of our friends out of the barn. Had she told somebody immediately, we would have had trouble, but instead she waited to meet you outside the barn."

"And you were waiting for us." Mark's voice was flat, emotionless.

"It was nothing personal, Mark. You certainly surprised me by surviving." The corner of Walter's mouth curved upward in a humorless smile. "And I must say, you have continued to surprise me, particularly by the acting ability you've exhibited. I must confess, you had me fooled. I thought I'd truly managed to scramble your brains with that shovel."

Mark lunged forward, as if to attack Walter. He was halted when Billy cocked his gun in warning and April grabbed his arm. "Damn you, Tilley. Damn you to hell," Mark cursed.

Walter looked at Billy. "Take them out and shoot them. Make sure their bodies aren't found for a very long time."

"What about her car?" Billy asked.

"I'll have Larry dispose of the car after they're taken care of." Walter turned to leave but was stopped at the door as Matthew entered.

"Hello, Walter," he said, his eyes as hard and cold as the gun he held. He stepped into the barn. "Having a party and forgot to invite me?"

"Matthew." For the first time since he'd arrived, Walter looked distressed. "How— What are you doing here?"

Johnna followed Matthew into the barn, a shotgun in her arms. "It isn't nice to walk out in the middle of a family meeting," she said.

Behind her, Luke sauntered in, a lazy smile curving his lips as he nodded to her, then to his brother.

April wanted to weep with gratitude. She wasn't sure exactly how the Delaneys had known she and Mark were in trouble, but she'd never been so happy to see anyone.

"Give the gun to Mark, Billy," Matthew instructed. At the same time Luke ascended the stairs to the loft.

Billy hesitated, sheer panic on his face. He pointed his gun first at Matthew, then at Mark.

"Give it up, Billy," Mark said softly. "It's over. Right now you aren't facing murder charges, but pull that trigger and one way or the other, your life is over."

"You shoot my brother, and trust me, your life is definitely over," Johnna said, her gun leveled at Billy.

With a scowl Billy handed Mark his gun. At the same time Luke escorted the illegal aliens downstairs.

"How did you all figure it out?" Walter asked.

"We didn't know exactly what was going on, but we knew something was up," Matthew said. "There was no conceivable reason for you and Billy to have contact with each other, but I saw the two of you together several times."

"And I saw you talking to Larry Greco one day in town," Luke added. "Not smart, Walter. Didn't your mama ever tell you that you get judged by the company you keep?"

"We were already suspicious of you before Billy interrupted our meeting this morning and you high-tailed it out of the house," Matthew continued. "All we had to do was follow you."

"The only real surprise here is that Mark is apparently all right," Johnna said, her gaze on Mark.

Before anyone could say anything more, several car doors slammed shut.

"That will be the sheriff and his men," Matthew said. Before the words were fully out of his mouth, Sheriff Broder and four deputies entered the barn.

The next thirty minutes were a flurry of activity. Walter, Larry and Billy were all handcuffed, along with the five illegal aliens. They were loaded into awaiting cars and driven off.

It was only then that Mark pulled April against him in an embrace of relief. "It's over," he murmured into her hair.

She clung to him, tears blurring her vision as she was overcome with emotion. She felt as if she'd been riding a roller coaster for the past several hours, shooting up to the heights of joy with Mark's arms around her, then slamming downward to the depths of despair when she'd believed they were going to die.

Mark finally released her. "Why don't you take your car and go on back to your cottage. I need to talk to my family."

"Okay. We'll talk later?" she asked.

He nodded and April fought the desire to fall back into his arms. Instead, knowing he had things to discuss with his brothers and sister, April left the barn and found her car where she and Mark had parked it hours before.

She drove back to her cottage, her heart filled with the sweet joy of love.

It was over. The bad guys were in custody, Mark no longer had to pretend brain damage, and everything was going to be just fine. The future was as bright and warm as the Inferno sun overhead.

Mark faced his family, both gratitude and shame coursing through him. "I have never been so grateful for family meetings," he said.

"I wondered where you were when I got up this morning," Matthew said. "Right before the meeting started, one of the hands came to tell me that your horse had come in earlier without you. Before I could do anything about that, Billy showed up and asked to speak to Walter. Yesterday you'd mentioned Billy to the sheriff and so when Walter and Billy left the house together, I knew something bad was going on."

"I always knew Walter was a slimeball," Johnna exclaimed. "But what I want to know is why you've been pretending to be brain damaged." There was a hard glint in Johnna's eyes as she glared at Mark.

"Am I the only one who didn't know that you were pretending?"

"Nobody knew...except April," Mark replied.

"You want to explain why you felt the need to fool us?" Matthew asked.

Mark sighed and raked a hand through his hair. "I thought it was the only way to find out what was going on around here."

"But why didn't you let us know what you were doing?" Johnna asked. Her eyes widened with sudden enlightenment. "You thought one of us might be involved, didn't you? You just didn't trust us enough to tell us the truth."

Mark's face warmed with shame as he thought of how he'd suspected one of his siblings of being involved in illegal activities, of killing Marietta and trying to kill him. "That night, just before Marietta was killed, she told me to trust nobody...not any of you and not the sheriff. She didn't know who was involved in all this."

"But *you* should have known," Johnna replied. "You should have known in your heart that none of us was involved in this. For goodness sake, Mark, we're your family!"

"It's one hell of a family we've got here, isn't it?" Luke said dryly. "Tell the truth, Johnna, if you'd been in Mark's place, would you have trusted the rest of us?"

Johnna leaned against the wall and sighed. "I don't know," she admitted. "It's sad, isn't it? That the four of us don't even really know one another."

"Father's legacy," Mark said with a touch of bitterness.

"Maybe the smartest thing we all should do is cut our losses and move on," Johnna said.

"And let Aunt Clara have everything?" Luke looked horrified. "That woman once dressed me in a bunny suit, for crying out loud."

Laughter erupted from all of them. Mark grinned at the memory. Luke had been about four, and Aunt Clara had come to the ranch for one of her frequent visits. It had been Easter time, and she'd brought a fuzzy white one-piece bunny suit for little Luke.

"We just worked together and managed to stop Walter from destroying the ranch. We can't just give up on each other now," Matthew said.

They eyed one another, and Mark knew they were all weighing their options, as he was. "We'll need to find another lawyer to oversee the terms of father's will. And there are half a dozen ranch hands who need to be fired for a variety of reasons." Mark swept a hand through his hair. "Somehow I just feel like if we let it all go, then he wins. From the grave our father manages to keep us from being a real family."

Even as he spoke the words, Mark wasn't sure if he and his brothers and sister could really learn to be a family. Their father certainly hadn't given them the tools to forge healthy relationships with one another, or with anyone.

April. Her name caused an ache in his heart. He loved her. And he knew it was time to put some distance between them. He loved her, but he didn't intend to do anything about it and he couldn't lead her on anymore.

Johnna pushed herself off the wall. "I don't know about the rest of you, but I need some time to think.

At the moment I'm hurt and angry that Mark didn't trust me. And I'm shocked by Walter's betrayal. I need some time to assess everything.''

"Why don't we have a family meeting in two days?" Matthew suggested. "In the meantime, I'll contact a lawyer, and Mark and I can start firing some men who apparently need to be fired.''

Johnna nodded, and together she and Luke left the barn.

''Come on, I'll give you a ride back to the house,'' Matthew said.

Mark shook his head. ''I'll walk back. I've got some thinking to do.''

Together the two brothers stepped out into the bright sunshine. Matthew's horse nickered and pawed the ground and Matthew absently stroked her mane, his gaze lingering on Mark. ''You should have come to me when Marietta first mentioned trouble to you.''

Mark raised an eyebrow wryly. ''From what you said earlier, you had some suspicions of your own, but you didn't pass those suspicions on to me, Luke or Johnna.''

A whisper of a smile curved Matthew's thin lips. ''I guess we all suffer the same lack of trust in others. We'll have to work on that.'' With these final words, Matthew mounted his horse and rode off toward the ranch.

Mark took off walking in the same direction. The hot sun felt good and the air was wonderfully clean smelling after the hours of being cooped up in the hole.

He was going to break April's heart. The knowledge of what he was about to do made his footsteps heavy. He loved April as he'd never loved anyone else in his life, but the conversation he'd just had with his siblings reinforced the perception that April would be better off without him.

April deserved a man who knew how to be a husband, a man who would know how to parent her son. She deserved more than what Mark could ever give her.

Making love to her had been a selfish indulgence on his part. He'd known with each kiss, every caress that he couldn't be the man for her, and yet he'd refused to deny himself the pleasure of loving her. And in this selfishness, he wondered if perhaps he was more like his father than he cared to admit.

As the cottages came into sight, dread filled Mark. He knew the most difficult thing he would ever do in his life was to stand before April and tell her that although he loved her, he could have no future with her.

When he reached April's place, Brian, Ricky and Doreen stood on the porch. "Hi, Mark," Brian greeted him, his eyes dancing with excitement. "Everyone is talking about you and Mom and how you caught the bad guys red-handed!"

"We saw the sheriff and the deputies taking the bad guys away," Ricky added. "And they told us that you and Brian's mom were heroes!"

Mark looked at Brian. "Where is your mom?"

"She's inside taking a quick shower." It was Doreen who replied. "She should be out in just a minute. I'm so grateful you're both all right."

"Yeah, me, too." Mark smiled. "Thankfully the Delaney cavalry arrived just in time."

At that moment April opened the door and stepped out on the porch. "Mark." She smiled her joy at seeing him, and her beauty made him ache inside.

"We need to talk," he said, then cast a self-conscious glance at Doreen and the two boys.

"Come on, guys, let's go to our place and rustle up some lunch," Doreen said.

Mark smiled gratefully. He needed to talk to April now, but certainly couldn't say what he needed to say in front of an audience.

"Come in," April said to him, a wrinkle of concern digging into her forehead. She opened the door to admit him into the cottage.

As he walked past her, he smelled the sweet, clean scent of her, and again his heart ached. She sat on the sofa and patted the space next to her. "What's wrong, Mark?" The wrinkle in her forehead deepened.

He sat next to her, his gaze focused on the wall across from them. He realized there was no way he could look into her lovely green eyes and tell her what he had to say.

"Mark?" She reached out and touched his hand, her fingers cool and trembling slightly. "What's wrong?"

He forced himself to look at her. "It was pretty scary there for a while, wasn't it?" She nodded, and he pulled his hand from hers. "But it's all over now."

"Yes," she said faintly, the worried wrinkle still creasing her forehead.

"I don't have to pretend anymore, and I need some time to put my life back in order." He looked away, not wanting to see the darkening of her eyes, the pain he knew his words would cause. "I think we need to cool it."

"Cool it?"

He sighed. "April, it's complicated—"

"What's complicated, Mark? I don't understand." Her voice trembled and her hands once again grabbed his. "Look at me, Mark. I need to tell you something." He did as she asked and looked at her once again. "I love you."

Her words stabbed through him like a bittersweet arrow. He wanted to sweep her up in his arms and hold her tight against him...and he wanted to run as fast as possible to escape the sweet yearning in those words.

Mark stood, unable to sit next to her and be strong. And, God help him, he had to be strong enough to walk away from her—for his sake, but, more important, for hers. "It ends here, April. I never had any intention of taking it as far as we did. I'm sorry if I hurt you."

"Hurt me?" Her lower lip trembled, and Mark fought the impulse to reach out to her, take her into his arms.

Mark paced back and forth, then stopped in front of her once again. "April, I told you I had no intention of ever being a husband and a father. I don't know how to be either. I had no role model. Hell, I can't even figure out how to be a family with my own brothers and sister."

April stood and took a step toward him. "Mark, that's not true. You'd make a wonderful father to Brian. I've watched you with him. And you'd make a wonderful husband to me."

Mark shook his head. "I'd only let you down. Rachel knew the truth. She knew I didn't have what it takes to have a family."

"I don't care what Rachel believed. Oh, Mark, don't fall into believing whatever your father said about you, what Rachel said about you. I know you, and I know you as the man I love, a man capable of loving me and Brian enough to build a lifetime of happiness." Her eyes shimmered with the force of her belief. "Don't let other people's expectations of you dictate what you'll be, what you'll have in your life."

Her words caused an ache inside Mark's heart, an ache of wistfulness, a wish that things were different, that he was different. But as he thought of Brian, so young and so needy, and he thought of his own upbringing, he knew with certainty that he wasn't the man to parent the boy.

He wasn't the man who could love April the way she deserved to be loved. He couldn't stand the thought of marrying her, then watching those lovely eyes of hers cloud with unhappiness as he somehow let her down again and again. "I'm sorry, April."

"Sorry?" Her cheeks flushed with color. "You know what I think? I think you did suffer some brain damage when Walter hit you with that shovel." She was angry, and Mark knew it was an anger born of pain.

"You think because you had a bad father, you'll be a bad father. You think because your family was messed up, you can't make a family of your own." Tears now glistened in her eyes. "You're wrong, Mark. Dead wrong. You are in charge of your future. Only you decide what kind of man you are and what you're capable of.'' She broke off and swiped her eyes angrily.

''I'm sorry,'' he repeated again, not knowing what else to say.

''What a fool I've been.'' She sat back down on the sofa. ''That first night we made love, I remember thinking that I didn't have anything left to lose by making love to you. Derrick had stolen my trust, my father had lost all my money.'' Her eyes burned into his. ''I was wrong. I had something else to lose. My heart.''

Mark turned and left, not knowing what else to say, unable to speak around his own heartbreak.

Chapter 14

April had believed no man could ever hurt her again, but she'd been wrong. Neither Derrick nor her father had hurt her as deeply, as profoundly as Mark. And what hurt the most was the fact that she'd been so certain, had believed in her heart that Mark did love her but was afraid to embrace that love.

Now she no longer knew what to believe.

The desert, which she had begun to see as beautiful, now appeared barren, a heat-seared landscape that was as colorless and empty as her heart.

She couldn't even sustain a healthy dose of anger at Mark. He'd warned her from the very beginning that he wasn't marriage material. She'd gone into a relationship with him with her eyes wide open and with a seed of hope in her heart.

She'd arrived at the Delaney Dude Ranch with a heart that had been broken by Derrick and her father, a heart that had been patched together by the healing of time and distance. However, nothing had prepared her for the utter shattering her heart had sustained when Mark walked away.

She hadn't even been able to hang on to her pride. Instead of letting him walk out the door, she had clung to him and professed her love for him.

For the next two days, April functioned by rote, doing her job, caring for Brian and trying to ignore the pain that thoughts of Mark brought with them.

Thankfully, she didn't see him in those two days. She knew the sight of him would only inflame the wounds he'd left in her heart and so she was grateful that their paths didn't cross.

She thought about leaving the ranch, packing up her car and heading for a place where her heart wouldn't be ripped apart each time she saw the man she loved. Ultimately, she knew she couldn't uproot Brian, who seemed happier than he'd ever been.

It was early morning on the third day after her talk with Mark when Doreen knocked on her door. April was still in her nightgown and had just started drinking her first cup of coffee.

"Good morning," she said in surprise and ushered Doreen into the kitchen.

"Hope you don't mind me dropping by so early," Doreen said, and nodded as April held up an empty cup. "Things have been so crazy the past couple of days, I don't feel like I've had a real chance to talk to you."

April knew much of the craziness Doreen mentioned had to do with the firing of half a dozen men from the ranch. She poured Doreen a cup of coffee, then joined her friend at the table. "Yes, it appears the Delaneys are doing some much-needed house-cleaning."

"I still can't believe Walter Tilley was running illegal aliens into the country through the ranch and murdered Marietta."

"I imagine he'll have lots of time in prison to think about his crimes."

"I also can't believe that Mark was only pretending to be brain damaged. He deserves an award for his performance." Speculation lit Doreen's gaze as it lingered on April. "But you knew that, didn't you?"

To April's horror, tears filled her eyes. She swiped at them quickly, but apparently not quickly enough. "Oh, April, I've upset you," Doreen said in dismay.

April wiped her eyes once again and shook her head. "No, you haven't upset me. Mark upset me." The last words eased out of her on a sigh of regret.

"You've fallen in love with him." It wasn't a question, but rather a statement of fact.

"Is it that obvious?" April asked, forcing a small, embarrassed laugh.

"Only to anyone with eyes to see. Anyone seeing you and Mark together would know there is a strong force of energy between the two of you."

"*Was* a strong force...or at least I thought there was, but no more." April willed the burning tears away, refusing to cry over Mark Delaney. "I love him, and I thought he loved me, but apparently I was mistaken. He is definitely a good actor." An edge of bitterness crept into her voice.

Doreen reached across the table and touched

April's hand. "I'm so sorry. Damn his handsome hide for breaking your heart."

April paused a moment to take a sip of her coffee. "The most difficult thing of all is that I believe he loves me. I believe it with every fiber of my being, but I think he's afraid to love me."

Doreen frowned. "Afraid? Why?"

"I'm not sure," April replied miserably. She traced the tip of a finger around the rim of her cup, her thoughts whirling in her head. "I think he's afraid that because his father was so terrible, he can't be a good father to Brian. I think he's scared that somehow he'll let me down, not be enough for me. I don't know...I only know that I love him and he's turned his back on any hope for a future together."

At that moment Brian opened his bedroom door and walked out. "'Morning," he mumbled sleepily.

"Good morning," April replied, hoping her son hadn't heard their conversation about Mark.

He walked over to one of the cabinets and withdrew a box of cereal. As he poured himself a bowl, Doreen stood.

"I'd better get back home before my munchkin wakes up and finds me gone." She looked at April with a sympathetic smile. "If you need to talk, you know where to find me."

April nodded. "Thanks, Doreen. We'll see you later."

It wasn't until Brian had finished his breakfast and left for the stables that April felt the first stir of anger deep within her. She embraced the emotion, finding it so much cleaner, so less painful than her heartache.

Damn his handsome hide for breaking your heart.

Doreen's words came back to her as she dressed for the day. Those words fueled the first stir of anger, building it and sustaining it.

Every time he'd kissed her with no intention of loving her, he'd cheated her. Every time he'd made love to her with no intention of loving her, he'd cheated her. He'd cheated them both.

Luke was the Delaney with the reputation as a womanizer, but apparently Luke could take lessons from his older brother.

What angered her the most was that she suspected he was allowing his father to dictate the kind of man he would be—a lonely, miserable man.

She finished dressing and left the cottage. The warmth of the Inferno sun reminded her of the heat of Mark's embrace. The rugged landscape of the desert was an aching reminder of Mark's strong shoulders.

Would there ever come a time when the very land that surrounded her didn't remind her of loving Mark? Would there ever come a time when she would forget the magic of his kisses, the passion they had shared?

She hoped so. She desperately hoped that eventually she could forget that she'd fallen in love with a wounded cowboy, one who couldn't get beyond the wounds of the past to embrace the future.

For Mark the past two days had been endless studies in torture. He'd spent most of the time alone in his house, thinking about his father, thinking about Rachel and ultimately thinking about April.

Thoughts of Rachel had stopped hurting a long time ago. He'd never loved Rachel, but rather had been willing to spend his life with her if that would please his father.

He had a feeling thoughts of his father would always yield pain. There were pieces of him that would never really heal, but that pain had at least become manageable.

It was the pain of the loss of April that ached inside him like an open sore. As he walked from room to room in his house, he kept imagining her presence there.

She would fill the place with her laughter, her scent...her love. She would bring flowers and knick-knacks, she'd transform the space within the walls from a house to a home.

It was easy to imagine Brian there, as well, spilling boyish energy through the rooms and claiming one of the spare rooms as his own territory.

As Mark walked toward the stables with the warmth of the morning sun on his shoulders, he told himself for the hundredth time that he'd done the right thing in cutting April loose.

But that didn't stop his arms from aching to hold her, didn't stop his heart from wishing that things might be different.

He entered the stable and shoved his disturbing thoughts aside. The scent of hay and leather, of horse-flesh and sawdust comforted him.

This was where he belonged, caring for the animals...animals who had no expectations, who would demand nothing of him that he couldn't give.

He braced himself as he heard the swish of a broom coming from one of the stables. He knew it would be Brian, doing his morning chores. He also knew seeing the boy would only make him once again think of April.

"Mark!" Brian leaned his broom against the wall when he spied Mark. "I've been waiting for you."

"You have?" Mark tried not to notice the eager pleasure that brightened Brian's features.

"You weren't here yesterday or the day before," Brian said, a small note of censure in his voice.

"Yeah, I had some things to do away from the stables." Mark walked from the stall where Brian had been sweeping to the tack room, Brian a shadow close behind him.

Mark took down a saddle that needed cleaning and oiling and set it on the railing used for that purpose. He was intensely aware of Brian standing close enough to him that he could smell the scent of boyhood that clung to him.

"Mark, could I talk to you?" Brian moved closer to him, so near Mark could feel the heat that radiated from his body. He could feel the intensity of the boy, as well, and knew whatever Brian wanted to say was obviously important.

Mark pulled up a stool, sat down and gave Brian his full attention. "What's up?"

Brian looked him straight in the eye. "I heard my mom and Ricky's mom talking this morning."

Mark tensed, wondering what Brian had overheard. "You did?"

Brian nodded. "Mom told Ricky's mom that she thought you were kinda scared to be a dad, and I just wanted to tell you there's nothing to be scared about."

A lump the size of a boulder rose up in the back

of Mark's throat as Brian grabbed his hand. "I know you got hit in the head and you don't think you're real smart," Brian continued. "But you don't have to be real smart to be a dad."

Mark's throat constricted as Brian's fingers tightened around his. "I mean, if you aren't sure you're doing it right, I could tell you. Mom and me, we could make sure you're doing it right. You already do most things a good dad would do." Brian's eyes gazed into Mark's with an innocent earnestness. "And I'd be a real easy son. I wouldn't sass you or be bad."

"Brian." Mark finally managed to talk, to breathe around the lump in his throat.

"You don't have to say anything now," Brian said as he released Mark's hand. "I just wanted to tell you that, so if you decide you want to marry my mom and be my dad, you'd know it's okay. I love you, Mark, and I think you'd be a real good dad." Apparently finished, Brian left the tack room.

Long after the boy had gone, Mark's fingers still burned with the imprint of his touch, and his words reverberated in his head.

The offer to help Mark, to be a good son, had been the sweet plea of a needy boy, and Mark would have to be a mountain to remain unmoved by the touching offer. *I love you, Mark, and I think you'd be a real good dad.* Emotion stuck in Mark's chest as Brian's words went around and around in his head.

And in that offer of help, in that confession of love, Mark saw the promise of all the things he could have with April and Brian. A family, laughter and tears, a future filled with love and the kind of life experiences that bond a couple forever.

For the first time he realized exactly what he was turning his back on, exactly what he was walking away from, and the ache inside him grew to mammoth proportions.

By noon, Mark had to get out of the stables. Strangely, working with the animals brought him no comfort.

Confusion swirled in his head. He wasn't confused about his love for April—that was the one thing shining and true. But, for the first time since walking away from her, he wondered if perhaps he wasn't making the biggest mistake of his life.

He got into his truck and headed for town, unsure what he intended, but knowing he needed to get away from the ranch.

The sun beat in through the window, warming his face and reminding him of the warmth of April nestled in his arms. He remembered how when he'd first met her, her eyes had reminded him of spring, of the promise of new life and hope.

Was he turning his back on spring and damning himself to a life of cold, barren winter? If his decision to cut himself off from April was so right, then why did it feel so wrong?

He parked his truck in front of his sister's law office and stared at the door. Never before in his life had he sought out one of his siblings to discuss a problem. But now he wanted to talk to Johnna about April. He needed to talk to his sister about the woman he loved.

He got out of his truck and entered the door to the law office. A secretary greeted him with a bright smile. "Hi, may I help you?"

A shaft of shame shot through Mark. His sister had opened this law office a year before, and he'd never been here before. The fact that her secretary didn't recognize him underscored the distance between himself and his sister.

"I'd like to see Johnna. Tell her that her brother is here."

The door to the left of the secretary's desk flew open and Johnna peered out. "Mark?" Her features radiated astonishment. "Come on in." She waved him toward her inner sanctum.

"Is everything all right? Did something happen at the ranch? Are Matthew and Luke okay?" She shot questions of concern at him as he eased down in the chair across from her desk.

"Matthew and Luke are fine. Nothing is wrong at the ranch."

She sat down at the desk facing him, lines of bewilderment still creasing her forehead. "Mark, what are you doing here?"

"Can't I visit my sister at her place of work? By the way, nice office."

She eyed him in disbelief. "I've been here a little over a year and none of my brothers has bothered to stop by."

"Then I guess my visit was overdue," Mark replied. Now that he was here, he was unsure how to even begin baring his heart.

Johnna leaned forward, her gray eyes watching him intently. "Mark, what's really going on?" she asked softly.

Mark leaned back in the chair and raked a hand through his hair, seeking the words that would unburden his heart. "You ever wonder why none of us is married? Or even in a relationship?"

Her eyes darkened with shadows of pain. "I know the reasons I'm not married or in a relationship, but I hadn't thought much about you three." She smiled tightly. "I guess I just figured in the back of my mind that you were all too bullheaded and difficult to fall in love."

"Even bullheaded men fall in love," Mark said.

"April." Johnna said her name without surprise. "How did you know?"

This time a full-bodied smile curved Johnna's lips. "It was pretty obvious how the two of you felt about each other in the old barn the other day. And it's been pretty obvious she's crazy about you from the first moment I met her. So, what do you intend to do about it?"

"Three days ago I told her I needed some time away from her, that nothing was going to come from our relationship."

Johnna sat forward and frowned. "And why in the hell would you do that if you love her?"

Again Mark raked a hand through his hair and averted his gaze from his sister. "Fear," he confessed. "Growing up, Dad always told me I wasn't good for much. How can a man who isn't good for much be a good husband? How can a man who didn't have a good father become one?" He looked at her again, knowing the depth of his torment was in his eyes for her to see.

"Oh, Mark." Johnna leaned back once again and sighed. "Dad left behind a lot of baggage for us to carry, didn't he? Matthew grows more difficult every day and continues to try to be the perfect son, I'm still so angry I can't get past it, and Luke pretends he has no pain by playing his guitar and romancing every single woman in town."

"We're a mess," Mark agreed.

"But how long do we continue being Father's victims? How long do we allow him to dictate our lives?"

She got up from her desk and crouched in front of Mark and took his hands in hers. "I can't tell you what to do. But I will tell you this—I had a chance at love once, and I allowed my temper and my own weaknesses to ruin that chance." Her eyes darkened with pain.

Mark knew she was talking about Jerrod McCain, the man who'd been the father to the baby she miscarried. Mark had never known what had happened between Johnna and Jerrod. He only knew that one day Jerrod had left town and Johnna had hardened.

"If fate is giving you a chance at love, don't throw it away." She squeezed his hands. "You're a good man, Mark. And whether you're a success or a failure as a husband and father is entirely up to you."

Mark stood and pulled his sister into his arms for an embrace. She'd said exactly what he'd wanted, needed to hear, what his heart had been trying to tell him all along.

"Thanks, Johnna," he said as he released her.

"This is the first time I can ever remember you talking to me about something that really matters."

He grinned. "Maybe there's hope for us Delaneys after all."

She nodded. "It's a beginning, isn't it?"

"Yeah, now I have to find out if I've ruined the other beginning I want."

"Go." Johnna smiled. "That woman is crazy about you. Don't let her get away."

Mark grinned and left the office. As he drove back to the ranch, his heart raced with anxiety. He knew exactly what he needed to do now. He only hoped it wasn't too late.

April left her office in the main house and started toward her cottage. It had been an excruciatingly long day. The guests seemed to be more demanding than usual, and she'd scarcely had a moment to think. Although thought was the last thing she wanted, her thoughts always went to Mark and what might have been.

She had begun to realize that she'd been wrong all along, that Mark had never really loved her at all. He'd desired her, lusted for her, but once that desire had been slaked, he'd been done. She'd mistaken his lust for love.

What hurt her most was that once again she'd managed to fall in love with a man seemingly incapable of returning her love.

She was a fool, but never again. She would build her life around Brian and forget about the romantic love she'd found so elusive.

She breathed a sigh of relief as her cottage came into sight and she saw Brian sitting on the front stoop waiting for her. "Hi, sport," she said.

"Hi, Mom."

"Did you get your chores done today?" she asked.

He nodded. "My room is all clean and I took out the garbage."

"Thanks, honey. Dinner will be ready in about half an hour, so don't go too far."

She entered the cottage, exhaustion weighing heavily. It wasn't a physical tiredness, she knew, rather a soul weariness. Despite her heartbreak, this was beginning to feel like home.

"Mom!" Brian called to her from outside the cottage. "Mom, come outside, I want to show you something."

April stepped out onto the porch. Instantly a rope swirled through the air and fell around her, effectively trapping her arms against her sides.

"You got her, Mark!" Brian jumped up and down and clapped his hands.

April stumbled forward as Mark began to tug on the rope, pulling her closer and closer to where he stood. "Let me go," she demanded.

"Nope." Mark continued to pull on the rope until she was standing directly in front of him. Before she could guess his intention, he picked her up and threw her over his shoulder.

"Put me down," she yelled, and drummed her fists into his broad back, outraged by his caveman antics.

"I'll put you down when I'm good and ready," he returned. He placed her in the saddle on the back of his horse, then mounted behind her. "Brian, you stay inside the cottage, and we'll be back in just a little while."

"Okay, Mark." He waved as Mark urged the horse forward.

"Let me down," April fumed as they rode across

the desert. "I'll have you arrested for kidnapping and I'm going to ground that traitor of a son of mine for the rest of his life."

He laughed. "Judge Wellsby would never throw me in jail for matters of the heart, and I talked Brian into helping me, so you can't punish him."

"You're crazy," she exclaimed.

"I am," he agreed. "I figured you'd still be too angry to hear me out, and I wanted to talk to you."

She knew where he was taking her, and she didn't say another word to him until they pulled up in front of his house. "Now you can just turn this horse around and take me back," she said.

"Not yet." He got off the horse, then reached up to help her down. "There's something I want you to see." Gently he removed the rope from her arms, and she steeled herself against the pleasure of his simplest touch.

Although she didn't want to be here with him, didn't want to talk to him, she was the tiniest bit curious about what he wanted her to see. She would see what he had to show her, then she'd demand he take her home.

As far as she was concerned, there was no going back. She was not giving Mark Delaney another chance to hurt her.

"You know what this is?" Mark walked over and placed his hand on top of a white post that jutted up from the ground.

"I have no idea," she replied and crossed her arms over her chest.

He frowned. She was so closed off, so obviously

clammed up against him. Despair swept through him.
Now that he'd allowed his feelings for her to bloom
fully inside him, he couldn't imagine his life without
her. But had he hurt her so deeply, she couldn't get
past that hurt?

"It's the beginning of a white picket fence."

She remained obviously unmoved. "You think you
can stick a post in the ground and that makes everything all right?" She frowned. "What are you hoping? That I'll say I love you and we'll tumble into
bed for a passionate hour or so?"

He swept off his hat with a touch of irritation. He
couldn't believe she thought this was all about a quick
tumble in bed. "This isn't about sex, April. If it were,
then I would never have told you I needed time away
from you."

"Then what are you doing, Mark?" Her voice held
a weary edge that drove his despair to a higher peak.

He walked over to the porch and sat down, then
patted the space next to him. She remained where she
was standing. His heart ached as he realized she
didn't intend to give him an inch. Her eyes were dull
pools of pain, and he only prayed that he hadn't dealt
their love a killing blow when he'd told her he needed
some distance, when he hadn't responded to her telling him she loved him.

He set his hat behind him and leaned forward, his
eyes boring into hers. "What am I doing? I can tell
you that for years I've struggled to be the perfect son,
to be so perfect I would finally earn my father's love
and respect. When I met you I was trying to be the
perfect hero, saving the ranch from the bad guys without any help from anyone."

He drew a deep breath, remembering how hard he'd tried to be perfect for his father and how he'd always been judged inadequate by the cold, harsh man. He now realized the inadequacies had not been in him, but rather in the man he'd tried so desperately to please.

Mark leaned back, shoving aside thoughts of his father. "It took your very bright son to make me realize the truth of things."

"Brian?" She stepped closer to where he sat.

Mark nodded and smiled, the memory of Brian's words warming him. "He came into the stable this morning and wanted to have a talk with me."

April frowned. "I guess he knows something has been going on between us and he's missed seeing you around our cottage for the past couple of days. I'm sorry if he bothered you."

"He didn't bother me. He cleared my head." Mark raced a hand through his hair, his gaze once again intent on her. "He thought maybe I was afraid that I was too dumb to be a father to him. He wanted to assure me that he'd help me be a good father, that together it would be okay."

He saw the slight shimmer of tears in April's eyes, the first hint of emotion she'd displayed. She wiped the tears and joined Mark on the porch. "I'm sorry if he pressured you in any way. He's just a kid. He doesn't understand adult relationships."

"No, he made me think." Mark took April's hand in his. She tried to pull it away, but he held tight. He wanted her to feel the love that radiated from him, know that only truth was falling from his lips. Her sweet floral scent surrounded him, and his heart raced with the possibility of spending the rest of his life loving her.

"After Brian talked to me, I drove into town and spoke with Johnna. But the whole time I was talking to her, it was Brian's words that kept echoing in my head."

"I don't understand," April confessed.

"After we got out of that hole, and I realized how much I loved you, it scared the hell out of me." He released her hand, stood and began to pace in front of where she sat. "What did I know about love? I'd had damn little while growing up. My family is so dysfunctional, I thought one of my siblings might have tried to kill me." Shame coursed through him at this confession. He stopped pacing and looked at her once again. "How could I possibly build a family of my own?"

She said nothing, although the skepticism in her eyes had faded and the tension that had given her a closed, unaccepting look was gone.

"But Brian made me realize something so important, so profound, it's taken all my fear away." He walked back out to where the post stood. "This is the start of a white picket fence. Three days ago I thought I had to build it all alone, that I had to be everything—the perfect man, the perfect husband and the perfect father—and I knew ultimately I couldn't be that. And that's why I told you we needed to cool it, to stop seeing each other. Because I knew I couldn't be everything to you."

"But nobody can be everything for anyone else. And nobody can be perfect all the time," April protested.

He nodded. "I know that now. Johnna asked me this afternoon how long I intended to be my father's victim, and I realized at that moment that I was tired of allowing myself to believe my father's limitations of me."

He walked back to where she sat and pulled her up to a standing position before him. "I love you, April, and I want you to be my wife." Mark's heart felt as if it might explode from his chest as he tried desperately to read her expression. "I can't promise you an easy life with no problems," he continued. "My brothers and sister can be difficult, ranching is hard work, and I'm going to make mistakes. I don't even know if next week the Delaney Dude Ranch will still be running. But I know I can't live without you."

Again her eyes grew luminous with tears, but Mark didn't know if the tears were ones of happiness or the forerunner of his own heartbreak.

He held her by the shoulders. "With your love and help, and Brian's love and help, I think the three of us can build us a fine picket fence." He held his breath and waited.

"You don't have to offer me a life of no problems. And you don't have to build me a picket fence." She reached up and wound her arms around his neck. "All you have to do is promise to love me forever."

"I do...and I will." He embraced her at the same time his lips hungrily claimed hers.

The Inferno heat that surrounded them felt tepid in comparison to the sparks of passion, the flames of love their kiss contained.

The ice that had encased April's heart for the past three days melted away beneath the kiss. When he'd first dropped that rope around her and carried her off on his horse, she'd been afraid to accept anything he had to say to her. She wasn't willing to risk her heart yet again.

But with Mark's lips on hers and his arms holding her tight, there was simply no room for fear in her heart. It was too filled with love for him.

"Marry me, April," he whispered as he broke the kiss. "Marry me and be my wife. I want you and Brian to be my family."

"Yes, oh, yes, Mark."

He kissed her again. This time the kiss was filled with promise, with hope, with the future. "We'd better get back to the cottage," he said with a touch of reluctance. "Brian will be waiting for us."

The fact that his thoughts were of her son only cemented the rightness of loving him. Tears once again filled her eyes as she thought of her son's love for Mark and Brian's incredible need for a father and a complete family.

She touched his cheek lovingly. "You're going to be an awesome father."

His eyes flashed, and the smile that lit his features soared into her heart. "I intend to be an awesome husband, as well."

The look in his eyes stole her breath away and caused a shiver of anticipation to race up her spine. Yes, he was going to be an awesome husband.

"We'll have a short engagement. Is that okay with you?" he asked, and she knew he felt the same as she did.

"As far as I'm concerned, a day-long engagement is too long."

He kissed her again, a long, lingering kiss that left her breathless and hungry for more. He released her, and grabbed his hat from the porch and plopped it on her head. "Come on, let's go tell Brian he's about to acquire a new father."

He helped her onto the horse and mounted behind her. She leaned into him, loving the way his body felt so close to hers. He wrapped his arms around her, holding her tight as they started back at a leisurely pace.

"Who would have thought," she mused, snuggling back against him.

"Who would have thought what?" he asked.

"When I first arrived here, I thought I'd been cast into hell. Who would have thought I'd find a piece of heaven to call my very own."

Mark's arms tightened around her and he kissed the side of her neck. "Who would have thought," he replied.

"Who would have thought what?" she asked.

"That a slow-witted cowboy who always felt like the invisible middle son would be the first to find love and happiness?"

April half turned in the saddle, so she could see his beautiful face. "You were never invisible to me."

"I love you, April." He swept his hands to gesture toward the land that surrounded them. "And I'll love you for as long as the sun shines on Inferno, for as long as those distant mountains remain. I'll do whatever I can to make you happy."

"All you have to do to make me happy is love me," she replied. "And promise to kiss me beneath a coyote moon every once in a while."

''That's a promise,'' he replied, his voice husky with love.

She leaned back against him once again, and in the warmth and strength of his arms she knew she was finally home.

* * * * *

THE DELANEY HEIRS

series will continue.
But first, catch Carla Cassidy's
contribution to
the ROYALLY WED *series,*

AN OFFICER AND A PRINCESS,

available in June
from Silhouette Romance.

Spines will tingle…mysteries await…
and dangerous passion lurks in the night
as Silhouette presents

DREAM SCAPES!

Thrills and chills abound in these four romances
welcoming readers to the dark side of love.
Available May 2001 at your favorite retail outlet:

IMMINENT THUNDER
by Rachel Lee

STRANGER IN THE MIST
by Lee Karr

FLASHBACK
by Terri Herrington

NOW AND FOREVER
by Kimberly Raye

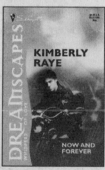

Meet 50 loving dads in

& BACHELORS USA
Take 4 FREE BOOKS,
Plus get a FREE GIFT!

Babies & Bachelors USA is a heartwarming new collection of reissued novels featuring 50 sexy heroes from every state who experience the ups and downs of fatherhood and find time for love all the same. All of the books, hand-picked by our editors, are outstanding romances by some of the world's bestselling authors, including Stella Bagwell, Kristine Rolofson, Judith Arnold and Marie Ferrarella!

Don't delay, order today! Call customer service at
1-800-873-8635.
Or
Clip this page and mail to The Reader Service:

In U.S.A.
P.O. Box 9049
Buffalo, NY
14269-9049

In CANADA
P.O. Box 616
Fort Erie, Ontario
L2A 5X3

YES! Please send me four FREE BOOKS and FREE GIFT along with the next four novels on a 14-day free home preview. If I like the books and decide to keep them, I'll pay just $15.96* U.S. or $18.00* CAN., and there's no charge for shipping and handling. Otherwise, I'll keep the 4 FREE BOOKS and FREE GIFT and return the rest. If I decide to continue, I'll receive six books each month—two of which are always free—until I've received the entire collection. In other words, if I collect all 50 volumes I will have paid for 32 and received 18 absolutely free!

267 HCK 4537
467 HCK 4538

Name	(Please Print)		
Address			Apt. #
City		State/Prov.	Zip/Postal Code

* Terms and prices subject to change without notice.
   Sales Tax applicable in N.Y. Canadian residents will be charged applicable provincial taxes
   and GST. All orders are subject to approval.

DIRBAB02   © 2000 Harlequin Enterprises Limited

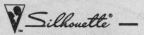
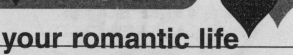

SILHOUETTE® MAKES YOU A STAR!

Look in the back pages of all June Silhouette series books to find an exciting new contest with fabulous prizes! Available exclusively through Silhouette.

Don't miss it!

Silhouette®
Where love comes alive™

P.S. Watch for details on how you can meet your favorite Silhouette author.

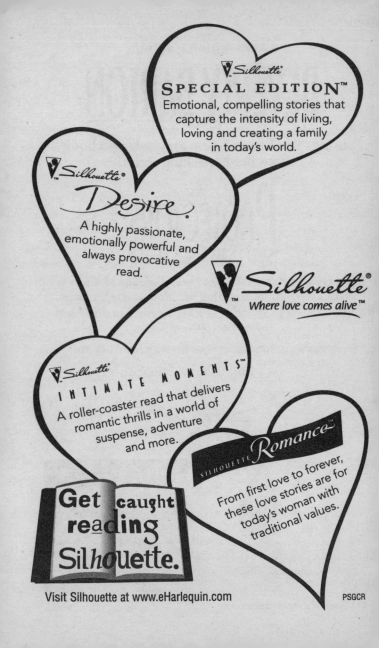